The Crocodile
and Other Tales

The Crocodile

and Other Tales

Fyodor Dostoevsky

WILDSIDE PRESS
Doylestown, Pennsylvania

Introduction copyright © 2003 Amy Sterling Casil.

The Crocodile and Other Tales
A publication of
Wildside Press
P.O. Box 301
Holicong, PA 18928-0301

www.wildsidepress.com

Table of Contents

INTRODUCTION. 7

THE CROCODILE 13
A GENTLE SPIRIT 59
THE LITTLE ORPHAN 117
THE PEASANT MAREY 125
THE DREAM OF A RIDICULOUS MAN 133
BOBOK 159

Introduction
By Amy Sterling Casil

There are many stories told of Fyodor Dostoevsky's life. Some are true, and some are not. It is clear that he suffered from some form of epilepsy; readers can parse the way he draws epileptic symptoms, such as the "aura" that precedes seizures, in novels like *The Idiot*. It is said that Dostoevsky's father, a rigid and unbending man, was murdered by his own serfs on the family's country estate. The truth is that his father died of "apoplexy" or a stroke.

His first novel, *Poor Folk*, was published in 1846. It was at this time that he joined the Petrashevsky circle of radical intellectuals. This association led to his arrest in 1849. Along with a group of his friends, he was imprisoned, eventually being led out for execution by order of the brutal Tsar Nicholas I. in Semyonovsky Square. At the last minute, he was reprieved. The execution was so realistic that two of his friends went insane. This experience of certain death colored all his later work. He then spent four years at hard labor in Siberia; this experience can be seen in the narrator's imprisonment and dreams of freedom represented in "The Peasant Marey." Educated as an engineer, Dostoevsky also spent four years in enforced military service; these Siberian years caused his health to deteriorate. As his writing strengthened, his epilepsy worsened.

Those who have not read much Dostoevsky, or who have only read the leaden early translations into English, which completely miss the character, and most importantly the humor of his writing, often associate him with later existentialist writers like Sartre and Gide. It is also important to have a sense of the Russian idea of holiness. When Dostoevsky wrote *The Idiot*, he said that he was struggling to write the story of "a truly good man" and there are strong parallels between "The Idiot" Prince Myshkin and Christ himself.

Dostoevsky is revered in Russia similarly to Tolstoy. Dostoevsky is a far flashier writer than Tolstoy, his points are generally more subtle, and yet his characters are in turn broader and wilder — sometimes extreme.

Those who have read only *Crime and Punishment* might be surprised to read "The Crocodile," in which the unnamed, downtrodden narrator feels secret glee at the predicament of his longtime "cultured friend" Ivan Matveich. The narrator, Ivan, and Ivan's wife the sugarplum Elena Ivanova visit the crocodile on exhibit in the Arcade. "Karlchen," the crocodile, is the pride and joy of his German owner. Filled with ripe satire of the horrible Russian economic state at the time, as well as wretched German, it is perhaps not surprising that "Karlchen" swallows pompous Ivan Matveich whole (Karlchen's insides are like a huge sack made of gutta-percha).

"You will, if Karlchen wird burst, therefore pay, das war mein Sohn, das war mein einziger Sohn," blurts the German owner as he argues with his wife and the temporarily unsettled Elena Ivanova. *That was my son! My only son!*

Ivan Matveich is hardly discomforted; speaking from inside the crocodile, he shares his megolamaniacal plans with the narrator. Meanwhile, the narrator has his eye on the juicy Elena Ivanova, and what a surprise it is when the narrator goes to Ivan's fellow government functionary for assistance. And the end is pure Dostoevsky, for the papers cannot agree as to just what meaning the crocodile in the arcade has, but most certainly – they are unsympathetic to Ivan Matveich.

"A Gentle Spirit" is not a "fantastic story." It is instead the story of a tragic misalliance between a dishonored and penurious, yet dreamy pawnbroker of forty-one years and his sixteen-year old enforced bride. With the strange, eldritch quality of many of Dostoevsky's women, the pawnbroker spins his tale of his young bride to its tragic end.

"The Little Orphan" is an exquisite short tale, reminiscent of Oscar Wilde's "The Selfish Giant," yet far more realistic, for there really were little orphan boys in the Petersburg of Dostoevsky's day.

The twenty-nine year old narrator of "The Peasant Marey" is imprisoned during Easter Week, remembering a time when he was nine, and a magical encounter with a strange and saintly peasant known only as "Marey." In this story are echoed both Dostoevsky's own years of imprisonment and suffering, and his lifelong love of the Russian land and peasant.

" . . . anyone would try to reassure a child, but here in this solitary encounter something quite different had happened, and had I been his very own son he could not have looked at me with a glance that radiated more pure love, and who had prompted him to do that? He was our own serf, and I was his master's little boy; no one would learn of his kindness to me and reward him for it."

The ridiculous narrator of "The Dream of A Ridiculous Man" imagines that he will kill himself, but by chance, falls asleep and merely dreams that he shoots himself with his hard-bought revolver. He dreams of a utopia — that he destroys. Carried outside of his body, believing himself to be dead, he visits an edenic planet.

"But their knowledge was higher and deeper than ours; for our science seeks to explain what life is, aspires to understand it in order to teach others how to love, while they without science knew how to live."

By his mere presence, he corrupts them.

"Like a vile trichina, like a germ of the plague infecting whole kingdoms, so I contaminated all this earth, so happy and sinless before my coming. They learnt to lie, grew fond of lying, and discovered the charm of falsehood."

Eventually he is transported back to his rooms; he becomes a preacher. Of course, everyone believes him to be utterly mad — but how ridiculous is he?

"Literary man" Ivan Ivanovitch is so ugly that his friend paints his picture and displays it at the Academy. Ivan reads the review: "Go and look at that morbid face suggesting insanity." Quite a realistic writer, Ivan cannot sell a novel though he has written one; his articles are all turned down. In a funk, he visits a funeral for entertainment. Impressed into carrying the coffin, he is appalled by the wretched condition of the graveyard. And sitting on a gravestone, the dead suddenly begin to speak.

They do not speak wisdom; in fact, they are continuing a sort of semi-life that echoes real life beyond the grave. Yet, they are depraved! They finally decide that they should not be telling lies, since lies are the way of the world up above — and rakish Klinevitch suggests they should just tear their bonds up and all go naked.

"Let us be naked, let us be naked!" cried all the voices.
"I long to be naked, I long to be," Avdotya Ignatyevna shrilled.

Of course Ivan's luck cannot hold. The "Bobek" or small bean of the title is a refrain that he hears; as the dead "age" in the ground, they gradually lose their faculties, finally falling truly dead. He sneezes, and the whole scene falls silent.

These stories, like Dostoevsky's writing, reflect the grief of living, and the impossibility of achieving salvation on earth.

The great writer himself died in 1881, having been in poor health for several years. Like Tolstoy, his funeral was attended by many thousands. It is often said that Dostoevsky was one of the first realists, and possessed a great understanding of psychology. Stories like "A Gentle Spirit" probe the relations between men and women in painful depth. Yet more, if one reads Dostoevsky, it was not so much the human mind in which he was expert, but the human spirit: passionate, ever-striving, yet so easily led astray.

Amy Sterling Casil
March, 2003
Woodland Hills, CA

The Crocodile
An Extraordinary Incident*

A true story of how a gentleman of a certain age and of respectable appearance was swallowed alive by the crocodile in the Arcade, and of the consequences that followed.

Ohe Lambert! Ou est Lambert?
As-tu vu Lambert?

I

ON the thirteenth of January of this present year, 1865, at half-past twelve in the day, Elena Ivanovna,

---

* Translated by Constance Garnett

the wife of my cultured friend Ivan Matveitch, who is a colleague in the same department, and may be said to be a distant relation of mine, too, expressed the desire to see the crocodile now on view at a fixed charge in the Arcade. As Ivan Matveitch had already in his pocket his ticket for a tour abroad (not so much for the sake of his health as for the improvement of his mind), and was consequently free from his official duties and had nothing whatever to do that morning, he offered no objection to his wife's irresistible fancy, but was positively aflame with curiosity himself.

"A capital idea!" he said, with the utmost satisfaction. "We'll have a look at the crocodile! On the eve of visiting Europe it is as well to acquaint ourselves on the spot with its indigenous inhabitants." And with these words, taking his wife's arm, he set off with her at once for the Arcade. I joined them, as I usually do, being an intimate friend of the family. I have never seen Ivan Matveitch in a more agreeable frame of mind than he was on that memorable morning — how true it is that we know not beforehand the fate that awaits us! On entering the Arcade he was at once full of admiration for the splendors of the building and, when we reached the shop in which the monster lately arrived in Petersburg was being exhibited, he volunteered to pay the quarter-ruble for me to the crocodile owner — a thing which had never happened before. Walking into a little room, we observed that besides the crocodile there were in it parrots of the species known as cockatoo, and also a group of monkeys in a special case in a recess. Near the entrance, along the left wall stood a big tin tank that looked like a bath covered with a thin iron grating, filled with water to the depth of two inches. In this shallow pool was kept a huge crocodile, which lay like a log absolutely motionless and apparently deprived of all its faculties by our damp climate, so inhospitable to foreign visitors. This monster at first aroused no special interest in any one of us.

"So this is the crocodile!" said Elena Ivanovna, with a pathetic cadence of regret. "Why, I thought it was . . . something different."

Most probably she thought it was made of diamonds. The owner of the crocodile, a German, came out and looked at us with an air of extraordinary pride.

"He has a right to be," Ivan Matveitch whispered to me, "he knows he is the only man in Russia exhibiting a crocodile."

This quite nonsensical observation I ascribe also to the extremely good-humored mood which had overtaken Ivan Matveitch, who was on other occasions of rather envious disposition.

"I fancy your crocodile is not alive," said Elena Ivanovna, piqued by the irresponsive stolidity of the proprietor, and addressing him with a charming smile in order to soften his churlishness — a maneuver so typically feminine.

"Oh, no, madam," the latter replied in broken Russian; and instantly moving the grating half off the tank, he poked the monster's head with a stick.

Then the treacherous monster, to show that it was alive, faintly stirred its paws and tail, raised its snout and emitted something like a prolonged snuffle.

"Come, don't be cross, Karlchen," said the German caressingly, gratified in his vanity.

"How horrid that crocodile is! I am really frightened," Elena Ivanovna twittered, still more coquettishly. "I know I shall dream of him now."

"But he won't bite you if you do dream of him," the German retorted gallantly, and was the first to laugh at his own jest, but none of us responded.

"Come, Semyon Semyonitch," said Elena Ivanovna,

addressing me exclusively, "let us go and look at the monkeys. I am awfully fond of monkeys; they are such darlings . . . and the crocodile is horrid."

"Oh, don't be afraid, my dear!" Ivan Matveitch called after us, gallantly displaying his manly courage to his wife. "This drowsy denizen of the realms of the Pharaohs will do us no harm." And he remained by the tank. What is more, he took his glove and began tickling the crocodile's nose with it, wishing, as he said afterwards, to induce him to snort. The proprietor showed his politeness to a lady by following Elena Ivanovna to the case of monkeys.

So everything was going well, and nothing could have been foreseen. Elena Ivanovna was quite skittish in her raptures over the monkeys, and seemed completely taken up with them. With shrieks of delight she was continually turning to me, as though determined not to notice the proprietor, and kept gushing with laughter at the resemblance she detected between these monkeys and her intimate friends and acquaintances. I, too, was amused, for the resemblance was unmistakable. The German did not know whether to laugh or not, and so at last was reduced to frowning. And it was at that moment that a terrible, I may say unnatural, scream set the room vibrating. Not knowing what to think, for the first moment I stood still, numb with horror, but, noticing that Elena Ivanovna was screaming too, I quickly turned round — and what did I behold! I saw — oh, heavens! — I saw the luckless Ivan Matveitch in the terrible jaws of the crocodile, held by them round the waist, lifted horizontally in the air and desperately kicking. Then — one moment, and no trace remained of him. But I must describe it in detail, for I stood all the while motionless, and had time to watch the whole process taking place before me with an attention and interest such as I never remember to have felt before. "What," I thought at that critical moment, "what if all that had happened to me instead of to Ivan Matveitch — how unpleasant it would have been for me!"

But to return to my story. The crocodile began by turning the unhappy Ivan Matveitch in his terrible jaws so that he could swallow his legs first; then bringing up Ivan Matveitch, who kept trying to jump out and clutching at the sides of the tank, sucked him down again as far as his waist. Then bringing him up again, gulped him down, and so again and again. In this way Ivan Matveitch was visibly disappearing before our eyes. At last, with a final gulp, the crocodile swallowed my cultured friend entirely, this time leaving no trace of him. From the outside of the crocodile we could see the protuberances of Ivan Matveitch's figure as he passed down the inside of the monster. I was on the point of screaming again when destiny played another treacherous trick upon us. The crocodile made a tremendous effort, probably oppressed by the magnitude of the object he had swallowed, once more opened his terrible jaws, and with a final hiccup he suddenly let the head of Ivan Matveitch pop out for a second, with an expression of despair on his face. In that brief instant the spectacles dropped off his nose to the bottom of the tank. It seemed as though that despairing countenance had only popped out to cast one last look on the objects around it, to take its last farewell of all earthly pleasures. But it had not time to carry out its intention; the crocodile made another effort, gave a gulp and instantly it vanished again — this time forever. This appearance and disappearance of a still living human head was so horrible, but all the same — either from its rapidity and unexpectedness or from the dropping of the spectacles — there was something so comic about it that I suddenly quite unexpectedly exploded with laughter. But pulling myself together and realizing that to laugh at such a moment was not the thing for an old family friend, I turned at once to Elena Ivanovna and said with a sympathetic air:

"Now it's all over with our friend Ivan Matveitch!"

I cannot even attempt to describe how violent was the agitation of Elena Ivanovna during the whole process. After the first scream she seemed rooted to the spot, and stared at the catastrophe with apparent indifference, though her eyes looked as though they were starting out of her head; then she suddenly went off into a heart-rending wail, but I seized her hands. At this instant the proprietor, too, who had at first been also petrified by horror, suddenly elapsed his hands and cried, gazing upwards:

"Oh, my crocodile! Oh, mein allerliebster Karlchen! Mutter, Mutter, Mutter!"

A door at the rear of the room opened at this cry, and the Mutter, a rosy-cheeked, elderly but disheveled woman in a cap made her appearance, and rushed with a shriek to her German.

A perfect Bedlam followed. Elena Ivanovna kept shrieking out the same phrase, as though in a frenzy, "Flay him! flay him!" apparently entreating them — probably in a moment of oblivion — to flay somebody for something. The proprietor and Mutter took no notice whatever of either of us; they were both bellowing like calves over the crocodile.

"He did for himself! He will burst himself at once, for he did swallow a ganz official!" cried the proprietor.

"Unser Karlchen, unser allerliebster Karlchen wird sterben," howled his wife.

"We are bereaved and without bread!" chimed in the proprietor.

"Flay him! flay him! flay him!" clamored Elena

Ivanovna, clutching at the German's coat.

"He did tease the crocodile. For what did your man tease the crocodile?" cried the German, pulling away from her. "You will, if Karlchen wird burst, therefore pay, das war mein Sohn, das war mein einziger Sohn."

I must own I was intensely indignant at the sight of such egoism in the German and the cold-heartedness of his disheveled Mutter; at the same time Elena Ivanovna's reiterated shriek of "Flay him! flay him!" troubled me even more and absorbed at last my whole attention, positively alarming me. I may as well say straight of that I entirely misunderstood this strange exclamation: it seemed to me that Elena Ivanovna had for the moment taken leave of her senses, but nevertheless wishing to avenge the loss of her beloved Ivan Matveitch, was demanding by way of compensation that the crocodile should be severely thrashed, while she was meaning something quite different. Looking round at the door, not without embarrassment, I began to entreat Elena Ivanovna to calm herself, and above all not to use the shocking word 'flay'. For such a reactionary desire here, in the midst of the Arcade and of the most cultured society, not two paces from the hall where at this very minute Mr. Lavrov was perhaps delivering a public lecture, was not only impossible but unthinkable, and might at any moment bring upon us the hisses of culture and the caricatures of Mr. Stepanov. To my horror I was immediately proved to be correct in my alarmed suspicions: the curtain that divided the crocodile room from the little entry where the quarter-rubles were taken suddenly parted, and in the opening there appeared a figure with moustaches and beard, carrying a cap, with the upper part of its body bent a long way forward, though the feet were scrupulously held beyond the threshold of the crocodile room in order to avoid the necessity of paying the entrance money.

"Such a reactionary desire, madam," said the stranger, trying to avoid falling over in our direction and to remain standing outside the room, "does no credit to your development, and is conditioned by lack of phosphorus in your brain. You will be promptly held up to shame in the Chronicle of Progress and in our satirical prints . . ."

But he could not complete his remarks; the proprietor coming to himself, and seeing with horror that a man was talking in the crocodile room without having paid entrance money, rushed furiously at the progressive stranger and turned him out with a punch from each fist. For a moment both vanished from our sight behind a curtain, and only then I grasped that the whole uproar was about nothing. Elena Ivanovna turned out quite innocent; she had, as I have mentioned already, no idea whatever of subjecting the crocodile to a degrading corporal punishment, and had simply expressed the desire that he should be opened and her husband released from his interior.

"What! You wish that my crocodile be perished!" the proprietor yelled, running in again. "No! let your husband be perished first, before my crocodile. . . ! Mein Vater showed crocodile, mein Grossvater showed crocodile, mein Sohn will show crocodile, and I will show crocodile! All will show crocodile! I am known to ganz Europa, and you are not known to ganz Europa, and you must pay me a Strafe!"

"Ja, ja," put in the vindictive German woman, "we shall not let you go, Strafe, since Karlchen is burst!"

"And, indeed, it's useless to flay the creature," I added calmly, anxious to get Elena Ivanovna away home as quickly as possible, "as our dear Ivan Matveitch is by now probably soaring somewhere in the empyrean."

"My dear" — we suddenly heard, to our intense amazement, the voice of Ivan Matveitch — "my dear, my advice is to apply direct to the superintendent's office, as without the assistance of the police the German will never be made to see reason."

These words, uttered with firmness and aplomb, and expressing an exceptional presence of mind, for the first minute so astounded us that we could not believe our ears. But, of course, we ran at once to the crocodile's tank, and with equal reverence and incredulity listened to the unhappy captive. His voice was muffled, thin and even squeaky, as though it came from a considerable distance. It reminded one of a jocose person who, covering his mouth with a pillow, shouts from an adjoining room, trying to mimic the sound of two peasants calling to one another in a deserted plain or across a wide ravine — a performance to which I once had the pleasure of listening in a friend's house at Christmas.

"Ivan Matveitch, my dear, and so you are alive!" faltered Elena Ivanovna.

"Alive and well," answered Ivan Matveitch, "and, thanks to the Almighty, swallowed without any damage whatever. I am only uneasy as to the view my superiors may take of the incident; for after getting a permit to go abroad I've got into a crocodile, which seems anything but clever."

"But, my dear, don't trouble your head about being clever; first of all we must somehow excavate you from where you are," Elena Ivanovna interrupted.

"Excavate!" cried the proprietor. "I will not let my crocodile be excavated. Now the Publican will come many more, and I will funfzig kopecks ask and Karlchen will cease to burst."

"Gott sei Dank!" put in his wife.

"They are right," Ivan Matveitch observed tranquilly; "the principles of economics before everything."

"My dear! I will fly at once to the authorities and lodge a complaint, for I feel that we cannot settle this mess by ourselves."

"I think so too." Observed Ivan Matveitch; "but in our age of industrial crisis it is not easy to rip open the belly of a crocodile without economic compensation, and meanwhile the inevitable question presents itself: What will the German take for his crocodile? And with it another: How will it be paid? For, as you know, I have no means . . ."

"Perhaps out of your salary . . ." I observed timidly, but the proprietor interrupted me at once.

"I will not the crocodile sell; I will for three thousand the crocodile sell! I will for four thousand the crocodile sell! Now the Publican will come very many. I will for five thousand the crocodile sell!"

In fact he gave himself insufferable airs. Covetousness and a revolting greed gleamed joyfully in his eyes.

"I am going!" I cried indignantly.

"And I! I too! I shall go to Andrey Osipitch himself. I will soften him with my tears," whined Elena Ivanovna.

"Don't do that, my dear," Ivan Matveitch hastened to interpose. He had long been jealous of Andrey Osipitch on his wife's account, and he knew she would enjoy going to weep before a gentleman of refinement, for tears suited her. "And I don't advise you to do so either, my friend," he added, addressing me. "It's no good plunging headlong in that slapdash way; there's no knowing what it may lead to. You had much better go today to Timofey Semyonitch, as though to pay an ordinary visit; he is an old-fashioned and by no means brilliant man, but he is trustworthy, and what matters most of all, he is straightforward. Give him my greetings and describe the circumstances of the case. And since I owe him seven rubles over our last game of cards, take the opportunity to pay him the money; that will soften the stern old man. In any case his advice may serve as a guide for us. And meanwhile take Elena Ivanovna home. . . . Calm yourself, my dear," he continued, addressing her. "I am weary of these outcries and feminine squabblings, and should like a nap. It's soft and warm in here, though I have hardly had time to look round in this unexpected haven."

"Look round! Why, is it light in there?" cried Elena Ivanovna in a tone of relief.

"I am surrounded by impenetrable night," answered the poor captive, "but I can feel and, so to speak, have a look round with my hands. . . . Good-bye; set your mind at rest and don't deny yourself recreation and diversion. Till tomorrow! And you, Semyon Semyonitch, come to me in the evening, and as you are absent-minded and may forget it, tie a knot in your handkerchief."

I confess I was glad to get away, for I was overtired and somewhat bored. Hastening to offer my arm to the disconsolate Elena Ivanovna, whose charms were only enhanced by her agitation, I hurriedly led her out of the crocodile room.

"The charge will be another quarter-ruble in the evening," the proprietor called after us.

"Oh, dear, how greedy they are!" said Elena Ivanovna, looking at herself in every mirror on the walls of the Arcade, and evidently aware that she was looking prettier than usual.

"The principles of economics," I answered with some emotion, proud that passers-by should see the lady on my arm.

"The principles of economics," she drawled in a touching little voice. "I did not in the least understand what Ivan Matveitch said about those horrid economics just now."

"I will explain to you," I answered, and began at once telling her of the beneficial effects of the introduction of foreign capital into our country, upon which I had read an article in the Petersburg News and the Voice that morning.

"How strange it is," she interrupted, after listening for some time. "But do leave off, you horrid man. What nonsense you are talking.... Tell me, do I look purple?"

"You look perfect, and not purple!" I observed, seizing the opportunity to pay her a compliment.

"Naughty man!" she said complacently. "Poor Ivan Matveitch," she added a minute later, putting her little head on one side coquettishly. "I am really sorry for him. Oh, dear!" she cried suddenly, "how is he going to have his dinner ... and ... and ... what will he do ... if he wants anything?"

"An unforeseen question," I answered, perplexed in my turn. To tell the truth, it had not entered my head, so much more practical are women than we men in the solution of the problems of daily life!

"Poor dear! how could he have got into such a mess ... nothing to amuse him, and in the dark. How vexing it is that I have no photograph of him. And so now I am a sort of widow," she added, with a seductive smile, evidently interested in her new position. "Hm...! I am sorry for him, though."

It was, in short, the expression of the very natural and intelligible grief of a young and interesting wife for the loss of her husband. I took her home at last, soothed her, and after dining with her and drinking a cup of aromatic coffee, set off at six o'clock to Timofey Semyonitch, calculating that at that hour all married people of settled habits would be sitting or lying down at home.

Having written this first chapter in a style appropriate to the incident recorded, I intended to proceed in a language more natural though less elevated, and I beg to forewarn the reader of the fact.

II

THE venerable Timofey Semyonitch met me rather nervously, as though somewhat embarrassed. He led me to his tiny study and shut the door carefully, "that the children may not hinder us," he added with evident uneasiness. There he made me sit down on a chair by the writing-table, sat down himself in an easy chair, wrapped round him the skirts of his old wadded dressing gown, and assumed an official and even severe air, in readiness for anything, though he was not my chief nor Ivan Matveitch's, and had hitherto been reckoned as a colleague and even a friend.

"First of all," he said, "take note that I am not a person in authority, but just such a subordinate official as you and Ivan Matveitch. . . . I have nothing to do with it, and do not intend to mix myself up in the affair."

I was surprised to find that he apparently knew all about it already. In spite of that I told him the whole story over in detail. I spoke with positive excitement, for I was at that moment fulfilling the obligations of a true friend. He listened without special surprise, but with evident signs of suspicion.

"Only fancy," he said, "I always believed that this would be sure to happen to him."

"Why, Timofey Semyonitch? It is a very unusual incident in itself . . ."

"I admit it. But Ivan Matveitch's whole career in the service was leading up to this end. He was flighty-conceited indeed. It was always 'progress' and ideas of all sorts, and this is what progress brings people to!"

"But this is a most unusual incident and cannot possibly serve as a general rule for all progressives."

"Yes, indeed it can. You see, it's the effect of overeducation, I assure you. For overeducation leads people to poke their noses into all sorts of places, especially where they are not invited. Though perhaps you know best," he added, as though offended. "I am an old man and not of much education. I began as a soldier's son, and this year has been the jubilee of my service."

"Oh, no, Timofey Semyonitch, not at all. On the contrary, Ivan Matveitch is eager for your advice; he is eager for your guidance. He implores it, so to say, with tears."

"So to say, with tears! Hm! Those are crocodile's tears and one cannot quite believe in them. Tell me, what possessed him to want to go abroad? And how could he afford to go? Why, he has no private means!"

"He had saved the money from his last bonus," I answered plaintively. "He only wanted to go for three months — to Switzerland . . . to the land of William Tell."

"William Tell? Hm!"

"He wanted to meet the spring at Naples, to see the museums, the customs, the animals . . ."

"Hm! The animals! I think it was simply from pride. What animals? Animals, indeed! Haven't we animals enough? We have museums, menageries, camels. There are bears quite close to Petersburg! And here he's got inside a crocodile himself . . ."

"Oh, come, Timofey Semyonitch! The man is in trouble, the man appeals to you as to a friend, as to an older relation, craves for advice — and you reproach him. Have pity at least on the unfortunate Elena Ivanovna!"

"You are speaking of his wife? A charming little lady," said Timofey Semyonitch, visibly softening and taking a pinch of snuff with relish. "Particularly prepossessing. And so plump, and always putting her pretty little head on one side. . . . Very agreeable. Andrey Osipitch was speaking of her only the other day."

"Speaking of her?"

"Yes, and in very flattering terms. Such a bust, he said, such eyes, such hair. . . . A sugar-plum, he said, not a lady — and then he laughed. He is still a young man, of course," Timofey Semyonitch blew his nose with a loud noise. "And yet, young though he is, what a career he is making for himself."

"That's quite a different thing, Timofey Semyonitch."

"Of course, of course."

"Well, what do You say then, Timofey Semyonitch?"

"Why, what can I do?"

"Give advice, guidance, as a man of experience, a relative! What are we to do? What steps are we to take? Go to the authorities and . . ."

"To the authorities? Certainly not." Timofey Semyonitch replied hurriedly. "If you ask my advice, you had better, above all, hush the matter up and act, so to speak, as a private person. It is a suspicious incident, quite unheard of. Unheard of, above all; there is no precedent for it, and it is far from creditable. . . . And so discretion above all. . . . Let him lie there a bit. We must wait and see. . . ."

"But how can we wait and see, Timofey Semyonitch?

What if he is stifled there?"

"Why should he be? I think you told me that he made himself fairly comfortable there?"

I told him the whole story over again. Timofey Semyonitch pondered.

"Hm!" he said, twisting his snuff-box in his hands. "To my mind it's really a good thing he should lie there a bit, instead of going abroad. Let him reflect at his leisure. Of course he mustn't be stifled, and so he must take measures to preserve his health, avoiding a cough, for instance, and so on. . . . And as for the German, it's my personal opinion he is within his rights, and even more so than the other side, because it was the other party who got into his crocodile without asking permission, and not he who got into Ivan Matveitch's crocodile without asking permission, though, so far as I recollect, the latter has no crocodile. And a crocodile is private property, and so it is impossible to slit him open without compensation."

"For the saving of human life, Timofey Semyonitch."

"Oh, well, that's a matter for the police. You must go to them."

"But Ivan Matveitch may be needed in the department. He may be asked for."

"Ivan Matveitch needed? Ha-ha! Besides, he is on leave, so that we may ignore him — let him inspect the countries of Europe! It will be a different matter if he doesn't turn up when his leave is over. Then we shall ask for him and make inquiries."

"Three months! Timofey Semyonitch, for pity's sake!"

"It's his own fault. Nobody thrust him there. At this rate we should have to get a nurse to look after him at government expense, and that is not allowed for in the regulations. But the chief point is that the crocodile is private property, so that the principles of economics apply in this question. And the principles of economics are paramount. Only the other evening, at Luke Andreitch's, Ignaty Prokofyitch was saying so. Do you know Ignaty Prokofyitch? A capitalist, in a big way of business, and he speaks so fluently. 'We need industrial development,' he said; 'there is very little development among us. We must create it. We must create capital, so we must create a middle class, the so-called bourgeoisie. And as we haven't capital we must attract it from abroad. We must, in the first place, give facilities to foreign companies to buy up lands in Russia as is done now abroad. The communal holding of land is poison, is ruin.' And, you know, he spoke with such heat; well, that's all right for him — a wealthy man, and not in the service. 'With the communal system,' he said, 'there will be no improvement in industrial development or agriculture. Foreign companies,' he said, 'must as far as possible buy up the whole of our land in big lots, and then split it up, split it up, split it up, in the smallest parts possible' — and do you know he pronounced the words 'split it up' with such determination — 'and then sell it as private property. Or rather, not sell it, but simply let it. When,' he said, 'all the land is in the hands of foreign companies they can fix any rent they like. And so the peasant will work three times as much for his daily bread and he can be turned out at pleasure. So that he will feel it, will be submissive and industrious, and will work three times as much for the same wages. But as it is, with the commune, what does he care? He knows he won't die of hunger, so he is lazy and drunken. And meanwhile money will be attracted into Russia, capital will be created and the bourgeoisie will spring up. The English political and literary paper, The Times, in an article the other day on our finances stated that the reason our financial position was so unsatisfactory was that we had no middle-class, no big fortunes, no accommodating proletariat.' Ignaty Prokofyitch speaks well. He is an orator. He wants to lay a report on the subject before the authorities, and then to get it published in the News. That's something very different from verses like Ivan Matveitch's . . ."

"But how about Ivan Matveitch?" I put in, after letting the old man babble on.

Timofey Semyonitch was sometimes fond of talking and showing that he was not behind the times, but knew all about things.

"How about Ivan Matveitch? Why, I am coming to that. Here we are, anxious to bring foreign capital into the country — and only consider: as soon as the capital of a foreigner, who has been attracted to Petersburg, has been doubled through Ivan Matvcitch, instead of protecting the foreign capitalist, we are proposing to rip open the belly of his original capital — the crocodile. Is it consistent? To my mind, Ivan Matveitch, as the true son of his fatherland, ought to rejoice and to be proud that through him the value of a foreign crocodile has been doubled and possibly even trebled. That's just what is wanted to attract capital. If one man succeeds, mind you, another will come with a crocodile, and a third will bring two or three of them at once, and capital will grow up about them — there you have a bourgeoisie. It must be encouraged."

"Upon my word, Timofey Semyonitch!" I cried, "you are demanding almost supernatural self-sacrifice from poor Ivan Matveitch."

"I demand nothing, and I beg you, before everything — as I have said already — to remember that I am not a person in authority and so cannot demand anything of anyone. I am speaking as a son of the fatherland, that is, not as the Son of the Fatherland, but as a son of the fatherland. Again, what possessed him to get into the crocodile? A respectable man, a man of good grade in the service, lawfully married — and then to behave like that! Is it consistent?"

"But it was an accident."

"Who knows? And where is the money to compensate the owner to come from?"

"Perhaps out of his salary, Timofey Semyonitch?"

"Would that be enough?"

"No, it wouldn't, Timofey Semyonitch," I answered sadly. "The proprietor was at first alarmed that the crocodile would burst, but as soon as he was sure that it was all right, he began to bluster and was delighted to think that he could double the charge for entry."

"Treble and quadruple perhaps! The public will simply stampede the place now, and crocodile owners are smart people. Besides, it's not Lent yet, and people are keen on diversions, and so I say again, the great thing is that Ivan Matveitch should preserve his incognito, don't let him be in a hurry. Let everybody know, perhaps, that he is in the crocodile, but don't let them be officially informed of it. Ivan Matveitch is in particularly favorable circumstances for that, for he is reckoned to be abroad. It will be said he is in the crocodile, and we will refuse to believe it. That is how it can be managed. The great thing is that he should wait; and why should he be in a hurry?"

"Well, but if . . ."

"Don't worry, he has a good constitution."

"Well, and afterwards, when he has waited?"

"Well, I won't conceal from you that the case is exceptional in the highest degree. One doesn't know what to think of it, and the worst of it is there is no precedent. If we had a precedent we might have something to go by. But as it is, what is one to say? It will certainly take time to settle it."

A happy thought flashed upon my mind.

"Cannot we arrange," I said, "that, if he is destined to remain in the entrails of the monster and it is the will of Providence that he should remain alive, he should send in a petition to be reckoned as still serving?"

"Hm. . . ! Possibly as on leave and without salary . . ."

"But couldn't it be with salary?"

"On what grounds?"

"As sent on a special commission."

"What commission and where?"

"Why, into the entrails, the entrails of the crocodile. . . . So to speak, for exploration, for investigation of the facts on the spot. It would, of course, be a novelty, but that is progressive and would at the same time show zeal for enlightenment."

Timofey Semyonitch thought a little.

"To send a special official," he said at last, "to the inside of a crocodile to conduct a special inquiry is, in my personal opinion, an absurdity. It is not in the regulations. And what sort of special inquiry could there be there?"

"The scientific study of nature on the spot, in the living subject. The natural sciences are all the fashion nowadays, botany. . . . He could live there and report his observations. . . . For instance, concerning digestion or simply habits. For the sake of accumulating facts."

"You mean as statistics. Well, I am no great authority on that subject, indeed I am no philosopher at all. You say 'facts' — we are overwhelmed with facts as it is, and don't know what to do with them. Besides, statistics are a danger."

"In what way?"

"They are a danger. Moreover, you will admit he will report facts, so to speak, lying like a log. And, can one do one's official duties lying like a log? That would be another novelty and a dangerous one; and again, there is no precedent for it. If we had any sort of precedent for it, then, to my thinking, he might have been given the job."

"But no live crocodiles have been brought over hitherto, Timofey Semyonitch."

"Hm . . . yes," he reflected again. "Your objection is a just one, if you like, and might indeed serve as a ground for carrying the matter further; but consider again, that if with the arrival of living crocodiles government clerks begin to disappear, and then on the ground that they are warm and comfortable there, expect to receive the official sanction for their position, and then take their ease there . . . you must admit it would be a bad example. We should have everyone trying to go the same way to get a salary for nothing."

"Do your best for him, Timofey Semyonitch. By the way, Ivan Matveitch asked me to give you seven rubles he had lost to you at cards."

"Ah, he lost that the other day at Nikifor Nikiforitch's. I remember. And how gay and amusing he was — and now!"

The old man was genuinely touched.

"Intercede for him, Timofey Semyonitch!"

"I will do my best. I will speak in my own name, as a private person, as though I were asking for information. And meanwhile, you find out indirectly, unofficially, how much would the proprietor consent to take for his crocodile?"

Timofey Semyonitch was visibly more friendly.

"Certainly," I answered. "And I will come back to you at once to report."

"And his wife . . . is she alone now? Is she depressed?"

"You should call on her, Timofey Semyonitch."

"I will. I thought of doing so before; it's a good

opportunity. . . . And what on earth possessed him to go and look at the crocodile. Though, indeed, I should like to see it myself."

"Go and see the poor fellow, Timofey Semyonitch."

"I will. Of course, I don't want to raise his hopes by doing so. I shall go as a private person. . . . Well, good-bye, I am going to Nikifor Nikiforitch's again; shall you be there?"

"No, I am going to see the poor prisoner."

"Yes, now he is a prisoner. . . ! Ah, that's what comes of thoughtlessness!"

I said good-bye to the old man. Ideas of all kinds were straying through my mind. A good-natured and most honest man, Timofey Semyonitch, yet, as I left him, I felt pleased at the thought that he had celebrated his fiftieth year of service, and that Timofey Semyonitchs are now a rarity among us. I flew at once, of course, to the Arcade to tell poor Ivan Matveitch all the news. And, indeed, I was moved by curiosity to know how he was getting on in the crocodile and how it was possible to live in a crocodile. And, indeed, was it possible to live in a crocodile at all? At times it really seemed to me as though it were all an outlandish, monstrous dream, especially as an outlandish monster was the chief figure in it.

III

AND yet it was not a dream, but actual, indubitable fact. Should I be telling the story if it were not? But to continue."

It was late, about nine o'clock, before I reached the Arcade, and I had to go into the crocodile room by the back entrance, for the German had closed the shop earlier than usual that evening. Now in the seclusion of domesticity he was walking about in a greasy old frock-coat, but he seemed three times as pleased as he had been in the morning. It was evidently that he had no apprehensions now, and that the public had been coming "many more." The Mutter came out later, evidently to keep an eye on me. The German and the Mutter frequently whispered together. Although the shop was closed he charged me a quarter-ruble. What unnecessary exactitude!

"You will every time pay; the public will one ruble, and you one quarter pay; for you are the good friend of your good friend; and I a friend respect . . ."

"Are you alive, are you alive, my cultured friend?" I cried, as I approached the crocodile, expecting my words to reach Ivan Matveitch from a distance and to flatter his vanity.

"Alive and well," he answered, as though from a long way off or from under the bed, though I was standing close beside him. "Alive and well; but of that later. . . . How are things going?"

As though purposely not hearing the question, I was just beginning with sympathetic haste to question him how he was, what it was like in the crocodile, and what, in fact, there was inside a crocodile. Both friendship and common civility demanded this. But with capricious annoyance he interrupted me.

"How are things going?" he shouted, in a shrill and on this occasion particularly revolting voice, addressing me peremptorily as usual.

I described to him my whole conversation with Timofey Semyonitch down to the smallest detail. As I told my story I tried to show my resentment in my voice.

"The old man is right," Ivan Matveitch pronounced as abruptly as usual in his conversation with me. "I like practical people, and can't endure sentimental milk-sops. I am ready to admit, however, that your idea about a special commission is not altogether absurd. I certainly have a great deal to report, both from a scientific and from an ethical point of view. But now all this has taken a new and unexpected aspect, and it is not worth while to trouble about mere salary. Listen attentively. Are you sitting down?"

"No, I am standing up."

"Sit down on the floor if there is nothing else, and listen attentively.

Resentfully I took a chair and put it down on the floor with a bang, in my anger.

"Listen," he began dictatorially. "The public came today in masses. There was no room left in the evening, and the police came in to keep order. At eight o'clock, that is, earlier than usual, the proprietor thought it necessary to close the shop and end the exhibition to count the money he had taken and prepare for tomorrow more conveniently. So I know there will be a regular fair tomorrow. So we may assume that all the most cultivated people in the capital, the ladies of the best society, the foreign ambassadors, the leading lawyers and so on, will all be present. What's more, people will be flowing here from the remotest provinces of our vast and interesting empire. The upshot of it is that I am the cynosure of all eyes, and though hidden to sight, I am eminent. I shall teach the idle crowd. Taught by experience, I shall be an example of greatness and resignation to fate! I shall be, so to say, a pulpit from which to instruct mankind. The mere biological details I can furnish about the monster I am inhabiting are of priceless value. And so, far from repining at what has happened, I confidently hope for the most brilliant of careers."

"You won't find it wearisome?" I asked sarcastically.

What irritated me more than anything was the extreme pomposity of his language. Nevertheless, it all rather disconcerted me. "What on earth, what, can this frivolous blockhead find to be so cocky about?" I muttered to myself. "He ought to be crying instead of being cocky."

"No!" he answered my observation sharply, "for I am full of great ideas, only now can I at leisure ponder over the amelioration of the lot of humanity. Truth and light will come forth now from the crocodile. I shall certainly develop a new economic theory of my own and I shall be proud of it — which I have hitherto been prevented from doing by my official duties and by trivial distractions. I shall refute everything and be a new Fourier. By the way, did you give Timofey Semyonitch the seven rubles?"

"Yes, out of my own pocket," I answered, trying to emphasize that fact in my voice.

"We will settle it," he answered superciliously. "I confidently expect my salary to be raised, for who should get a rise if not I? I am of the utmost service now. But to business, My wife?"

"You are, I suppose, inquiring after Elena Ivanovna?"

"My wife?" he shouted, this time in a positive squeal.

There was no help for it! Meekly, though gnashing my teeth, I told him how I had left Elena Ivanovna. He did not even hear me out.

"I have special plans in regard to her," he began impatiently. "If I am celebrated here, I wish her to be celebrated there. Savants, poets, philosophers, foreign mineralogists, statesmen, after conversing in the morning with me, will visit her salon in the evening. From next week onwards she must have an 'At Home' every evening. With my salary doubled, we shall have the means for entertaining, and as the entertainment must not go beyond tea and hired footmen — that's settled. Both here and there they will talk of me. I have long thirsted for an opportunity for being talked about, but could not attain it, fettered by my humble position and low grade in the service. And now all this has been attained by a simple gulp on the part of the crocodile. Every word of mine will be listened to, every utterance will be thought over, repeated, printed. And I'll teach them what I am worth! They shall understand at last what abilities they have allowed to vanish in the entrails of a monster. 'This man might have been Foreign Minister or might have ruled a kingdom,' some will say. 'And that man did not rule a kingdom,' others will say. In what way am I inferior to a Garnier-Pagesishky or whatever they are called? My wife must be a worthy second — I have brains, she has beauty and charm. 'She is beautiful, and that is why she is his wife,' some will say. 'She is beautiful because she is his wife,' others will amend. To be ready for anything let Elena Ivanovna buy tomorrow the Encyclopedia edited by Andrey Kraevsky, that she may be able to converse on any topic. Above all, let her be sure to read the political leader in the Petersburg News, comparing it every day with the Voice. I imagine that the proprietor will consent to take me sometimes with the crocodile to my wife's brilliant salon. I will be in a tank in the middle of the magnificent drawing room, and I will scintillate with witticisms which I will prepare in the morning. To the statesman I will impart my projects; to the poet I will speak in rhyme; with the ladies I can be amusing and charming without impropriety, since I shall be no danger to their husbands' peace of mind. To all the rest I shall serve as a pattern of resignation to fate and the will of Providence. I shall make my wife a brilliant literary lady; I shall bring her forward and explain her to the public; as my wife she must be full of the most striking virtues; and if they are right in calling Andrey Alexandrovitch our Russian Alfred de Musset, they will be still more right in calling her our Russian Yevgenia Tour."

I must confess that, although this wild nonsense was rather in Ivan Matveitch's habitual style, it did occur to me that he was in a fever and delirious. It was the same, everyday Ivan Matveitch, but magnified twenty times.

"My friend," I asked him, "are you hoping for a long life? Tell me, in fact, are you well? How do you eat, how do you sleep, how do you breathe? I am your friend, and you must admit that the incident is most unnatural, and consequently my curiosity is most natural."

"Idle curiosity and nothing else," he pronounced sententiously, "but you shall be satisfied. You ask how I am managing in the entrails of the monster? To begin with, the crocodile, to my amusement, turns out to be perfectly empty. His inside consists of a sort of huge empty sack made of gutta-percha, like the elastic goods sold in the Gorohovy Street, in the Morskaya, and, if I am not mistaken, in the Voznesensky Prospect. Otherwise, if you think of it, how could I find room?"

"Is it possible?" I cried, in a surprise that may well be understood. "Can the crocodile be perfectly empty?"

"Perfectly," Ivan Matveitch maintained sternly and impressively. "And in all probability, it is so constructed by the laws of Nature. The crocodile possesses nothing but jaws furnished with sharp teeth, and besides the jaws, a tail of considerable length — that is all, properly speaking. The middle part between these two extremities is an empty space enclosed by something of the nature of gutta-percha, probably really gutta-percha."

"But the ribs, the stomach, the intestines, the liver, the heart?" I interrupted quite angrily.

"There is nothing, absolutely nothing of all that, and probably there never has been. All that is the idle fancy of frivolous travelers. As one inflates an air-cushion, I am now with my person inflating the crocodile. He is incredibly elastic. Indeed, you might, as the friend of the family, get in with me if you were generous and self-sacrificing enough — and even with you here there would be room to spare. I even think that in the last resort I might send for Elena Ivanovna. However, this void, hollow formation of the crocodile is quite in keeping with the teachings of natural science. If, for instance, one had to construct a new crocodile, the question would naturally present itself. What is the fundamental characteristic of the crocodile? The answer is clear: to swallow human beings. How is one, in constructing the crocodile, to secure that he should swallow people? The answer is clearer still: construct him hollow. It was settled by physics long ago that Nature abhors a vacuum. Hence the inside of the crocodile must be hollow so that it may abhor the vacuum, and consequently swallow and so fill itself with anything it can come across. And that is the sole rational cause why every crocodile swallows men. It is not the same in the constitution of man: the emptier a man's head is, for instance, the less he feels the thirst to fill it, and that is the one exception to the general rule. It is all as clear as day to me now. I have deduced it by my own observation and experience, being, so to say, in the very bowels of Nature, in its retort, listening to the throbbing of its pulse. Even etymology supports me, for the very word crocodile means voracity. Crocodile — *crocodillo* — is evidently an Italian word, dating perhaps from the Egyptian Pharaohs, and evidently derived from the French verb croquer, which means to eat, to devour, in general to absorb nourishment. All these remarks I intend to deliver as my first lecture in Elena Ivanovna's salon when they take me there in the tank."

"My friend, oughtn't you at least to take some purgative?" I cried involuntarily.

"He is in a fever, a fever, he is feverish!" I repeated to myself in alarm.

"Nonsense!" he answered contemptuously. "Besides, in my present position it would be most inconvenient. I knew, though, you would be sure to talk of taking medicine."

"But, my friend, how... how do you take food now? Have you dined today?"

"No, but I am not hungry, and most likely I shall never take food again. And that, too, is quite natural; filling the whole interior of the crocodile I make him feel always full. Now he need not be fed for some years. On the other hand, nourished by me, he will naturally impart to me all the vital juices of his body; it is the same as with some accomplished coquettes who embed themselves and their whole persons for the night in raw steak, and then, after their morning bath, are fresh, supple, buxom and fascinating. In that way nourishing the crocodile, I myself obtain nourishment from him, consequently we mutually nourish one another. But as it is difficult even for a crocodile to digest a man like me, he must, no doubt, be conscious of a certain weight in his stomach — an organ which he does not, however, possess — and that is why, to avoid causing the creature suffering, I do not often turn over, and although I could turn over I do not do so from humanitarian motives. This is the one drawback of my present position, and in an allegorical sense Timofey Semyonitch was right in saying I was lying like a log. But I will prove that even lying like a log — nay, that only lying like a log — one can revolutionize the lot of mankind. All the great ideas and movements of our newspapers and magazines have evidently been the work of men who were lying like logs; that is why they call them divorced from the realities of life — but what does it matter, their saying that! I am constructing now a complete system of my own, and you wouldn't believe how easy it is! You have only to creep into a secluded corner or into a crocodile, to shut your eyes, and you immediately devise a perfect millennium for mankind. When you went away this afternoon I set to work at once and have already invented three systems, now I am preparing the fourth. It is true that at first one must refute everything that has gone before, but from the crocodile it is so easy to refute it; besides, it all becomes clearer, seen from the inside of the crocodile.... There are some drawbacks, though small ones, in my position, however; it is somewhat damp here and covered with a sort of slime; moreover, there is rather a smell of India-rubber exactly like the smell of my old galoshes. That is all, there are no other drawbacks."

"Ivan Matveitch," I interrupted, "all this is a miracle in which I can scarcely believe. And can you, can you intend never to dine again?"

"What trivial nonsense you are troubling about, you thoughtless, frivolous creature! I talk to you about great ideas, and you . . . Understand that I am sufficiently nourished by the great ideas which light up the darkness in which I am enveloped. The good-natured proprietor has, however, after consulting the kindly Mutter, decided with her that they will every morning insert into the monster's jaws a bent metal tube, something like a whistle pipe, by means of which I can absorb coffee or broth with bread soaked in it. The pipe has already been bespoken in the neighborhood, but I think this is superfluous luxury. I hope to live at least a thousand years, if it is true that crocodiles live so long, which, by the way — good thing I thought of it — you had better look up in some natural history tomorrow and tell me, for I may have been mistaken and have mixed it up with some excavated monster. There is only one reflection rather troubles me: as I am dressed in cloth and have boots on, the crocodile can obviously not digest me. Besides, I am alive, and so am opposing the process of digestion with my whole will power; for you can understand that I do not wish to be turned into what all nourishment turns into, for that would be too humiliating for me. But there is one thing I am afraid of: in a thousand years the cloth of my coat, unfortunately of Russian make, may decay, and then, left without clothing, I might perhaps, in spite of my indignation, begin to be digested; and though by day nothing would induce me to allow it, at night, in my sleep, when a man's will deserts him, I may be overtaken by the humiliating destiny of a potato, a pancake, or veal. Such an idea reduces me to fury. This alone is an argument for the revision of the tariff and the encouragement of the importation of English cloth, which is stronger and so will withstand Nature longer when one is swallowed by a crocodile. At the first opportunity I will impart this idea to some statesman and at the same time to the political writers on our Petersburg dailies. Let them publish it abroad. I trust this will not be the only idea they will borrow from me. I foresee that every morning a regular crowd of them, provided with quarter-rubles from the editorial office, will be flocking round me to seize my ideas on the telegrams of the previous day. In brief, the future presents itself to me in the rosiest light."

"Fever, fever!" I whispered to myself.

"My friend, and freedom?" I asked, wishing to learn his views thoroughly. "You are, so to speak, in prison, while every man has a right to the enjoyment of freedom."

"You are a fool," he answered. "Savages love independence, wise men love order; and if there is no order.

"Ivan Matveitch, spare me, please!"

"Hold your tongue and listen!" he squealed, vexed at my interrupting him. "Never has my spirit soared as now. In my narrow refuge there is only one thing that I dread — the literary criticisms of the monthlies and the lies of our satirical papers. I am afraid that thoughtless visitors, stupid and envious people and nihilists in general, may turn me into ridicule. But I will take measures. I am impatiently awaiting the response of the public tomorrow, and especially the opinion of the newspapers. You must tell me about the papers tomorrow."

"Very good; tomorrow I will bring a perfect pile of papers with me."

"Tomorrow it is too soon to expect reports in the newspapers, for it will take four days for it to be advertised. But from today come to me every evening by the back way through the yard. I am intending to employ you as my secretary. You shall read the newspapers and magazines to me, and I will dictate to you my ideas and give you commissions. Be particularly careful not to forget the foreign telegrams. Let all the European telegrams be here every day. But enough; most likely you are sleepy by now. Go home, and do not think of what I said just now about criticisms: I am not afraid of it, for the critics themselves are in a critical position. One has only to be wise and virtuous and one will certainly get on to a pedestal. If not Socrates, then Diogenes, or perhaps both of them together — that is my future role among mankind."

So frivolously and boastfully did Ivan Matveitch hasten to express himself before me, like feverish weak-willed women who, as we are told by the proverb, cannot keep a secret. All that he told me about the crocodile struck me as most suspicious. How was it possible that the crocodile was absolutely hollow? I don't mind betting that he was bragging from vanity and partly to humiliate me. It is true that he was an invalid and one must make allowances for invalids; but I must frankly confess, I never could endure Ivan Matveitch. I have been trying all my life, from a child up, to escape from his tutelage and have not been able to! A thousand times over I have been tempted to break with him altogether, and every time I have been drawn to him again, as though I were still hoping to prove something to him or to revenge myself on him. A strange thing, this friendship! I can positively assert that nine-tenths of my friendship for him was made up of malice. On this occasion, however, we parted with genuine feeling.

"Your friend a very clever man!" the German said to me in an undertone as he moved to see me out; he had been listening all the time attentively to our conversation.

"Apropos," I said, "while I think of it: how much would you ask for your crocodile in case anyone wanted to buy it?"

Ivan Matveitch, who heard the question, was waiting with curiosity for the answer; it was evident that he did not want the German to ask too little; anyway, he cleared his throat in a peculiar way on hearing my question.

At first the German would not listen — was positively angry.

"No one will dare my own crocodile to buy!" he cried furiously, and turned as red as a boiled lobster. "Me not want to sell the crocodile! I would not for the crocodile a million thalers take. I took a hundred and thirty thalers from the public today, and I shall tomorrow ten thousand take, and then a hundred thousand every day I shall take. I will not him sell."

Ivan Matveitch positively chuckled with satisfaction. Controlling myself — for I felt it was a duty to my friend — I hinted coolly and reasonably to the crazy German that his calculations were not quite correct, that if he makes a hundred thousand every day, all Petersburg will have visited him in four days, and then there will be no one left to bring him rubles, that life and death are in God's hands, that the crocodile may burst or Ivan Matveitch may fall ill and die, and so on and so on.

The German grew pensive.

"I will him drops from the chemist's get," he said, after pondering, "and will save your friend that he die not."

"Drops are all very well," I answered, "but consider, too, that the thing may get into the law courts. Ivan Matveitch's wife may demand the restitution of her lawful spouse. You are intending to get rich, but do you intend to give Elena Ivanovna a pension?"

"No, me not intend," said the German in stern decision.

"No, we not intend," said the Mutter, with positive malignancy.

"And so would it not be better for you to accept something now, at once, a secure and solid though moderate sum, than to leave things to chance? I ought to tell you that I am inquiring simply from curiosity."

The German drew the Mutter aside to consult with her in a corner where there stood a case with the largest and ugliest monkey of his collection.

"Well, you will see!" said Ivan Matveitch.

As for me, I was at that moment burning with the desire, first, to give the German a thrashing, next, to give the Mutter an even sounder one, and, thirdly, to give Ivan Matveitch the soundest thrashing of all for his boundless vanity. But all this paled beside the answer of the rapacious German.

After consultation with the Mutter he demanded for his crocodile fifty thousand rubles in bonds of the last Russian loan with lottery voucher attached, a brick house in Gorohovy Street with a chemist's shop attached, and in addition the rank of Russian colonel.

"You see!" Ivan Matveitch cried triumphantly. "I told you so! Apart from this last senseless desire for the rank of a colonel, he is perfectly right, for he fully understands the present value of the monster he is exhibiting. The economic principle before everything!"

"Upon my word!" I cried furiously to the German. "But what should you be made a colonel for? What exploit have you performed? What service have you done? In what way have you gained military glory? You are really crazy!"

"Crazy!" cried the German, offended. "No, a person very sensible, but you very stupid! I have a colonel deserved for that I have a crocodile shown and in him a live Hofrath sitting! And a Russian can a crocodile not show and a live Hofrath in him sitting! Me extremely clever man and much wish colonel to be!"

"Well, good-bye, then, Ivan Matveitch!" I cried, shaking with fury, and I went out of the crocodile room almost at a run.

I felt that in another minute I could not have answered for myself. The unnatural expectations of these two blockheads were insupportable. The cold air refreshed me and somewhat moderated my indignation. At last, after spitting vigorously fifteen times on each side, I took a cab, got home, undressed and flung myself into bed. What vexed me more than anything was my having become his secretary. Now I was to die of boredom there every evening, doing the duty of a true friend! I was ready to beat myself for it, and I did, in fact, after putting out the candle and pulling up the bedclothes, punch myself several times on the head and various parts of my body. That somewhat relieved me, and at last I fell asleep fairly soundly, in fact, for I was very tired. All night long I could dream of nothing but monkeys, but towards morning I dreamt of Elena Ivanovna.

IV

THE monkeys I dreamed about, I suppose, because they were shut up in the case at the German's; but Elena Ivanovna was a different story.

I may as well say at once, I loved the lady, but I make haste — post-haste — to make a qualification. I loved her as a father, neither more nor less. I judge that because I often felt an irresistible desire to kiss her little head or her rosy cheek. And though I never carried out this inclination, I would not have refused even to kiss her lips. And not merely her lips, but her teeth, which always gleamed so charmingly like two rows of pretty, well-matched pearls when she laughed. She laughed extraordinarily often. Ivan Matveitch in demonstrative moments used to call her his "darling absurdity" — a name extremely happy and appropriate. She was a perfect sugarplum, and that was all one could say of her. Therefore I am utterly at a loss to understand what possessed Ivan Matveitch to imagine his wife as a Russian Yevgenia Tour? Anyway, my dream, with the exception of the monkeys, left a most pleasant impression upon me, and going over all the incidents of the previous day as I drank my morning cup of tea, I resolved to go and see Elena Ivanovna at once on my way to the office — which, indeed, I was bound to do as the friend of the family.

In a tiny little room out of the bedroom — the so-called little drawing room, though their big drawing room was little too — Elena Ivanovna was sitting, in some half-transparent morning wrapper, on a smart little sofa before a little tea-table, drinking coffee out of a little cup in which she was dipping a minute biscuit. She was ravishingly pretty, but struck me as being at the same time rather pensive.

"Ah, that's you, naughty man!" she said, greeting me with an absent-minded smile. "Sit down, feather-head, have some coffee. Well, what were you doing yesterday? Were you at the masquerade?"

"Why, were you? I don't go, you know. Besides, yesterday I was visiting our captive . . . . . . I sighed and assumed a pious expression as I took the coffee.

"Whom. . . ? What captive. . . ? Oh, yes! Poor fellow! Well, how is he — bored? Do you know . . . I wanted to ask you . . . I suppose I can ask for a divorce now?"

"A divorce!" I cried in indignation and almost spilled the coffee. "It's that swarthy fellow," I thought to myself bitterly.

There was a certain swarthy gentleman with little moustaches who was something in the architectural fine, and who came far too often to see them, and was extremely skillful in amusing Elena Ivanovna. I must confess I hated him and there was no doubt that he had succeeded in seeing Elena Ivanovna yesterday either at the masquerade or even here, and putting all sorts of nonsense into her head.

"Why," Elena Ivanovna rattled off hurriedly, as though it were a lesson she had learnt, "if he is going to stay on in the crocodile, perhaps not come back all his life, while I sit waiting for him here! A husband ought to live at home, and not in a crocodile...."

"But this was an unforeseen occurrence," I was beginning, in very comprehensible agitation.

"Oh, no, don't talk to me, I won't listen, I won't listen," she cried, suddenly getting quite cross. "You are always against me, you wretch! There's no doing anything with you, you will never give me any advice! Other people tell me that I can get a divorce because Ivan Matveitch will not get his salary now."

"Elena Ivanovna! is it you I hear!" I exclaimed pathetically. "What villain could have put such an idea into your head? And divorce on such a trivial ground as a salary is quite impossible. And poor Ivan Matveitch, poor Ivan Matveitch is, so to speak, burning with love for you even in the bowels of the monster. What's more, he is melting away with love like a lump of sugar. Yesterday while you were enjoying yourself at the masquerade, he was saying that he might in the last resort send for you as his lawful spouse to join him in the entrails of the monster, especially as it appears the crocodile is exceedingly roomy, not only able to accommodate two but even three persons...."

And then I told her all that interesting part of my conversation the night before with Ivan Matveitch.

"What, what!" she cried, in surprise. "You want me to get into the monster too, to be with Ivan Matveitch? What an idea! And how am I to get in there, in my hat and crinoline? Heavens, what foolishness! And what should I look like while I was getting into it, and very likely there would be someone there to see me! It's absurd! And what should I have to eat there? And . . . and . . . and what should I do there when . . . Oh, my goodness, what will they think of next. . . ? And what should I have to amuse me there. . . ? You say there's a smell of gutta-percha? And what should I do if we quarreled — should we have to go on staying there side by side? Foo, how horrid!"

"I agree, I agree with all those arguments, my sweet Elena Ivanovna," I interrupted, striving to express myself with that natural enthusiasm which always overtakes a man when he feels the truth is on his side. "But one thing you have not appreciated in all this, you have not realized that he cannot live without you if he is inviting you there; that is a proof of love, passionate, faithful, ardent love. . . . You have thought too little of his love, dear Elena Ivanovna!"

"I won't, I won't, I won't hear anything about it!" waving me off with her pretty little hand with glistening pink nails that had just been washed and polished. "Horrid man! You will reduce me to tears! Get into it yourself, if you like the prospect. You are his friend, get in and keep him company, and spend your life discussing some tedious science. . . ."

"You are wrong to laugh at this suggestion" — I checked the frivolous woman with dignity — "Ivan Matveitch has invited me as it is. You, of course, are summoned there by duty; for me, it would be an act of generosity. But when Ivan Matveitch described to me last night the elasticity of the crocodile, he hinted very plainly that there would be room not only for you two, but for me also as a friend of the family, especially if I wished to join you, and therefore . . ."

"How so, the three of us?" cried Elena Ivanovna, looking at me in surprise. "Why, how should we . . . are we going to be all three there together? Ha-ha-ha!

How silly you both are! Ha-ha-ha ! I shall certainly pinch you all the time, you wretch! Ha-ha-ha! Ha-ha-ha!"

And falling back on the sofa, she laughed till she cried. All this — the tears and the laughter — were so fascinating that I could not resist rushing eagerly to kiss her hand, which she did not oppose, though she did pinch my cars lightly as a sign of reconciliation.

Then we both grew very cheerful, and I described to her in detail all Ivan Matveitch's plans. The thought of her evening receptions and her salon pleased her very much.

"Only I should need a great many new dresses," she observed, "and so Ivan Matveitch must send me as much of his salary as possible and as soon as possible. Only . . . only I don't know about that," she added thoughtfully. "How can he be brought here in the tank? That's very absurd. I don't want my husband to be carried about in a tank. I should feel quite ashamed for my visitors to see it. . . . I don't want that, no, I don't."

"By the way, while I think of it, was Timofey Semyonitch here yesterday?"

"Oh, yes, he was; he came to comfort me, and do you know, we played cards all the time. He played for sweetmeats, and if I lost he was to kiss my hands. What a wretch he is! And only fancy, he almost came to the masquerade with me, really!"

"He was carried away by his feelings!" I observed. "And who would not be with you, you charmer?"

"Oh, get along with your compliments! Stay, I'll give you a pinch as a parting present. I've learnt to pinch awfully well lately. Well, what do you say to that? By the way, you say Ivan Matveitch spoke several times of me yesterday?"

"N-no, not exactly. . . . I must say he is thinking

more now of the fate of humanity, and wants . . ."

"Oh, let him! You needn't go on! I am sure it's fearfully boring. I'll go and see him some time. I shall certainly go tomorrow. Only not today; I've got a headache, and besides, there will be such a lot of people there today. . . . They'll say, 'That's his wife,' and I shall feel ashamed. . . . Good-bye. You will be . . . there this evening, won't you?"

"To see him, yes. He asked me to go and take him the papers."

"That's capital. Go and read to him. But don't come and see me today. I am not well, and perhaps I may go and see someone. Good-bye, you naughty man."

"It's that swarthy fellow is going to see her this evening," I thought.

At the office, of course, I gave no sign of being consumed by these cares and anxieties. But soon I noticed some of the most progressive papers seemed to be passing particularly rapidly from hand to hand among my colleagues, and were being read with an extremely serious expression of face. The first one that reached me was the *News-sheet,* a paper of no particular party but humanitarian in general, for which it was regarded with contempt among us, though it was read. Not without surprise I read in it the following paragraph:

"Yesterday strange rumors were circulating among the spacious ways and sumptuous buildings of our vast metropolis. A certain well-known bon-vivant of the highest society, probably weary of the cuisine at Borel's and at the X. Club, went into the Arcade, into the place where an immense crocodile recently brought to the metropolis is being exhibited, and insisted on its being prepared for his dinner. After bargaining with the proprietor he at once set to work to devour him (that is, not the proprietor, a very meek and punctilious

German, but his crocodile), cutting juicy morsels with his penknife from the living animal, and swallowing them with extraordinary rapidity. By degrees the whole crocodile disappeared into the vast recesses of his stomach, so that he was even on the point of attacking an ichneumon, a constant companion of the crocodile, probably imagining that the latter would be as savory. We are by no means opposed to that new article of diet with which foreign gourmands have long been familiar. We have, indeed, predicted that it would come. English lords and travelers make up regular parties for catching crocodiles in Egypt, and consume the back of the monster cooked like beef-steak, with mustard, onions and potatoes. The French followed in the train of Lesseps prefer the paws baked in hot ashes, which they do, however, in opposition to the English, who laugh at them. Probably both ways would be appreciated among us. For our part, we are delighted at a new branch of industry, of which our great and varied fatherland stands pre-eminently in need. Probably before a year is out crocodiles will be brought in hundreds to replace this first one, lost in the stomach of a Petersburg gourmand. And why should not the crocodile be acclimatized among us in Russia? If the water of the Neva is too cold for these interesting strangers, there are ponds in the capital and rivers and lakes outside it. Why not breed crocodiles at Pargolovo, for instance, or at Pavlovsk, in the Presnensky Ponds and in Samoteka in Moscow? While providing agreeable, wholesome nourishment for our fastidious gourmands, they might at the same time entertain the ladies who walk about these ponds and instruct the children in natural history. The crocodile skin might be used for making jewel-cases, boxes, cigar-cases, pocketbooks, and possibly more than one thousand saved up in the greasy notes that are peculiarly beloved of merchants might be laid by in crocodile skin. We hope to return more than once to this interesting topic."

Though I had foreseen something of the sort, yet the reckless inaccuracy of the paragraph overwhelmed me. Finding no one with whom to share my impression, I turned to Prohor Savvitch who was sitting opposite to me, and noticed that the latter had been watching me for some time, while in his hand he held the Voice as though he were on the point of passing it to me. Without a word he took the *News-sheet* from me, and as he handed me the Voice he drew a line with his nail against an article to which he probably wished to call my attention. This Prohor Savvitch was a very queer man: a taciturn old bachelor, he was not on intimate terms with any of us, scarcely spoke to anyone in the office, always had an opinion of his own about everything, but could not bear to impart it to anyone. He lived alone. Hardly anyone among us had ever been in his lodging.

This was what I read in the Voice.

"Everyone knows that we are progressive and humanitarian and want to be on a level with Europe in this respect. But in spite of all our exertions and the efforts of our paper we are still far from maturity, as may be judged from the shocking incident which took place yesterday in the Arcade and which we predicted long ago. A foreigner arrives in the capital bringing with him a crocodile which he begins exhibiting in the Arcade. We immediately hasten to welcome a new branch of useful industry such as our powerful and varied fatherland stands in great need of. Suddenly yesterday at four o'clock in the afternoon a gentleman of exceptional stoutness enters the foreigner's shop in an intoxicated condition, pays his entrance money, and immediately without any warning leaps into the jaws of the crocodile, who was forced, of course, to swallow him, if only from an instinct of self-preservation, to avoid being crushed. Tumbling into the inside of the crocodile, the stranger at once dropped asleep. Neither the shouts of the foreign proprietor, nor the lamentations of his terrified family, nor threats to send for the police made the slightest impression. Within the crocodile was heard nothing but laughter and a promise to flay him (sic), though the poor mammal, compelled to swallow such a mass, was vainly shedding tears. An uninvited guest is worse than a Tartar. But in spite of the proverb the insolent visitor would not leave. We do not know how to explain such barbarous incidents which prove our lack of culture and disgrace us in the eyes of foreigners. The recklessness of the Russian temperament has found a fresh outlet. It may be asked what was the object of the uninvited visitor? A warm and comfortable abode? But there are many excellent houses in the capital with very cheap and comfortable lodgings, with the Neva water laid on, and a staircase lighted by gas, frequently with a hall-porter maintained by the proprietor. We would call our readers' attention to the barbarous treatment of domestic animals: it is difficult, of course, for the crocodile to digest such a mass all at once, and now he lies swollen out to the size of a mountain, awaiting death in insufferable agonies. In Europe persons guilty of inhumanity towards domestic animals have long been punished by law. But in spite of our European enlightenment, in spite of our European pavements, in spite of the European architecture of our houses, we are still far from shaking off our time-honored traditions.

"Though the houses are new, the conventions are old."

And, indeed, the houses are not new, at least the

staircases in them are not. We have more than once in our paper alluded to the fact that in the Petersburg Side in the house of the merchant Lukyanov the steps of the wooden staircase have decayed, fallen away, and have long been a danger for Afimya Skapidarov, a soldier's wife who works in the house, and is often obliged to go up the stairs with water or armfuls of wood. At last our predictions have come true: yesterday evening at half-past eight Afimya Skapidarov fell down with a basin of soup and broke her leg. We do not know whether Lukyanov will mend his staircase now, Russians are often wise after the event, but the victim of Russian carelessness has by now been taken to the hospital. In the same way we shall never cease to maintain that the house-porters who clear away the mud from the wooden pavement in the Viborgsky Side ought not to spatter the legs of passers-by, but should throw the mud up into heaps as is done in Europe," and so on, and so on.

"What's this?" I asked in some perplexity, looking at Prohor Savvitch. "What's the meaning of it?"

"How do you mean?"

"Why, upon my word! Instead of pitying Ivan Matveitch, they pity the crocodile!"

"What of it? They have pity even for a beast, a mammal. We must be up to Europe, mustn't we? They have a very warm feeling for crocodiles there too. He-he-he!"

Saying this, queer old Prohor Savvitch dived into his papers and would not utter another word.

I stuffed the Voice and the *News-sheet* into my pocket and collected as many old copies of the newspapers as I could find for Ivan Matveitch's diversion in the evening, and though the evening was far off, yet on this occasion I slipped away from the office early to go to the Arcade and look, if only from a distance, at what was going on there, and to listen to the various remarks and currents of opinion. I foresaw that there would be a regular crush there, and turned up the collar of my coat to meet it. I somehow felt rather shy — so unaccustomed are we to publicity. But I feel that I have no right to report my own prosaic feelings when faced with this remarkable and original incident.

A Gentle Spirit
*A Fantastic Story**

Part I
Chapter I
Who I was and who she was

Oh, while she is still here, it is still all right; I go up and look at her every minute; but tomorrow they will take her away — and how shall I be left alone? Now she is on the table in the drawing room, they put two card tables together, the coffin will be here tomorrow

* Translated by Constance Garnett.

— white, pure white "gros de Naples" — but that's not it . . .

I keep walking about, trying to explain it to myself. I have been trying for the last six hours to get it clear, but still I can't think of it all as a whole.

The fact is I walk to and fro, and to and fro.

This is how it was. I will simply tell it in order. (Order!)

Gentlemen, I am far from being a literary man and you will see that; but no matter, I'll tell it as I understand it myself. The horror of it for me is that I understand it all!

It was, if you care to know, that is to take it from the beginning, that she used to come to me simply to pawn things, to pay for advertising in the *voice* to the effect that a governess was quite willing to travel, to give lessons at home, and so on, and so on. That was at the very beginning, and I, of course, made no difference between her and the others: "She comes," I thought, "like anyone else," and so on.

But afterwards I began to see a difference. She was such a slender, fair little thing, rather tall, always a little awkward with me, as though embarrassed (I fancy she was the same with all strangers, and in her eyes, of course, I was exactly like anybody else — that is, not as a pawnbroker but as a man).

As soon as she received the money she would turn round at once and go away. And always in silence. Other women argue so, entreat, haggle for me to give them more; this one did not ask for more. . . .

I believe I am muddling it up.

Yes; I was struck first of all by the things she brought: poor little silver gilt earrings, a trashy little locket, things not worth sixpence. She knew herself that they were worth next to nothing, but I could see from her face that they were treasures to her, and I found out afterwards as a fact that they were all that was left her belonging to her father and mother.

Only once I allowed myself to scoff at her things. You see I never allow myself to behave like that. I keep up a gentlemanly tone with my clients: few words, politeness and severity. "Severity, severity!"

But once she ventured to bring her last rag, that is, literally the remains of an old hareskin jacket, and I could not resist saying something by way of a joke. My goodness! how she flared up! Her eyes were large, blue and dreamy but — how they blazed. But she did not drop one word; picking up her "rags" she walked out.

It was then for the first time I noticed her particularly, and thought something of the kind about her — that it, something of a particular kind. Yes, I remember another impression — that is, if you will have it, perhaps the chief impression, that summed up everything. It was that she was terribly young, so young that she looked just fourteen. And yet she was within three months of sixteen. I didn't mean that, though, that wasn't what summed it all up. Next day she came again. I found out later that she had been to Dobranravov's and to Mozer's with that jacket, but they take nothing but gold and would have nothing to say to it. I once took some stones from her (rubbishy little ones) and, thinking it over afterwards, I wondered: I, too, only lend on gold and silver, yet from her I accepted stones. That was my second thought about her then; that I remember. That time, that is when she came from Mozer's, she brought an amber cigar-holder. It was a connoisseur's article, not bad, but again, of no value to us, because we only deal in gold. As it was the day after her "mutiny," I received her sternly. Sternness with me takes the form of dryness. As I gave her two rubles, however, I could not resist saying, with a certain irritation, "I only do it for you, of course; Mozer wouldn't take such a thing."

The words "for you" I emphasized particularly, and with a particular implication.

I was spiteful. She flushed up again when she heard that "for you," but she did not say a word, she did not refuse the money, she took it — that is poverty! But how hotly she flushed! I saw I had stung her. And when she had gone out, I suddenly asked myself whether my triumph over her was worth two rubles. He! He!! He!!! I remember I put that question to myself twice over, "was is worth it? was it worth it?"

And, laughing, I inwardly answered it in the affirmative. And I felt very much elated. But that was not an evil feeling; I said it with design, with a motive; I wanted to test her, because certain ideas with regard to her had suddenly come into my mind. That was the third thing I thought particularly about her. . . . Well, it was from that time it all began. Of course, I tried at once to find out all her circumstances indirectly, and awaited her coming with a special impatience. I had a presentiment that she would come soon. When she came, I entered into affable conversation with her, speaking with unusual politeness. I have not been badly brought up and have manners. H'm. It was then I guessed that she was soft-hearted and gentle.

The gentle and soft-hearted do not resist long, and though they are by no means very ready to reveal themselves, they do not know how to escape from a conversation; they are niggardly in their answers, but they do answer, and the more readily the longer you go on. Only, on your side you must not flag, if you want them to talk. I need hardly say that she did not explain anything to me then. About the Voice and all that I found out afterwards. She was at that time spending her last farthing on advertising, haughtily at first, of course. "A governess prepared to travel and will send terms on application," but, later on: "willing to do anything, to teach, to be a companion, to be a housekeeper, to wait on an invalid, plain sewing, and so on, and so on," the usual thing! Of course, all this was added to the advertisement a bit at a time and finally, when she was reduced to despair, it came to: "without salary in return for board." No, she could not find a situation. I made up my mind then to test her for the last time. I suddenly took up the Voice of the day and showed her an advertisement. "A young person, without friends and relations, seeks a situation as a governess to young children, preferably in the family of a middle-aged widower. Might be a comfort in the home."

"Look here how this lady has advertised this morning, and by the evening she will certainly have found a situation. That's the way to advertise."

Again she flushed crimson and her eyes blazed, she turned round and went straight out. I was very much pleased, though by that time I felt sure of everything and had no apprehensions; nobody will take her cigar-holders, I thought. Besides, she has got rid of them all. And so it was, two days later, she came in again, such a pale little creature, all agitation — I saw that something had happened to her at home, and something really had. I will explain directly what had happened, but now I only want to recall how I did something chic, and rose in her opinion. I suddenly decided to do it. The fact is she was pawning the icon (she had brought herself to pawn it!) . . Ah! listen! listen! This is the beginning now, I've been in a muddle. You see I want to recall all this, every detail, every little point. I want to bring them all together and look at them as a whole and — I cannot . . . It's these little things, these little things. . . . It was an icon of the Madonna. A Madonna with the Babe, and old-fashioned, homely one, and the setting was silver gilt, worth — well, six rubles perhaps. I could see the icon was precious to her; she was pawning it whole, not taking it out of the setting. I said to her —

"You had better take it out of the setting, and take the icon home; for it's not the thing to pawn."

"Why, are you forbidden to take them?"

"No, it's not that we are forbidden, but you might, perhaps, yourself . . ."

"Well, take it out."

"I tell you what. I will not take it out, but I'll set it here in the shrine with the other icons," I said, on reflection. "Under the little lamp" (I always had the lamp burning as soon as the shop was opened), "and you simply take ten rubles."

"Don't give me ten rubles. I only want five; I shall certainly redeem it."

"You don't want ten? The icon's worth it," I added noticing that her eyes flashed again.

She was silent. I brought out five rubles.

"Don't despise anyone; I've been in such straits myself; and worse too, and that you see me here in this business . . . is owing to what I've been through in the past. . . ."

"You're revenging yourself on the world? Yes?" she interrupted suddenly with rather sarcastic mockery, which, however, was to a great extent innocent (that is, it was general, because certainly at that time she did not distinguish me from others, so that she said it almost without malice).

"Aha," thought I; "so that's what you're like. You've got character; you belong to the new movement."

"You see!" I remarked at once, half-jestingly, half-mysteriously, "I am part of that part of the Whole that seeks to do ill, but does good. . . ."

Quickly and with great curiosity, in which, however,

there was something very childlike, she looked at me.

"Stay... what's that idea? Where does it come from? I've heard it somewhere..."

"Don't rack your brains. In those words Mephistopheles introduces himself to Faust. Have you read Faust?"

"Not... not attentively."

"That is, you have not read it at all. You must read it. But I see an ironical look in your face again. Please don't imagine that I've so little taste as to try to use Mephistopheles to commend myself to you and grace the role of pawnbroker. A pawnbroker will still be a pawnbroker. We know."

"You're so strange... I didn't mean to say anything of that sort."

She meant to say: "I didn't expect to find you were an educated man"; but she didn't say it; I knew, though, that she thought that. I had pleased her very much.

"You see," I observed, "One may do good in any calling – I'm not speaking of myself, of course. Let us grant that I'm doing nothing but harm, yet..."

"Of course, one can do good in every position," she said, glancing at me with a rapid, profound look. "Yes, in any position," she added suddenly.

Oh, I remember, I remember all those moments! And I want to add, too, that when such young creatures, such sweet young creatures want to say something so clever and profound, they show at once so truthfully and naïvely in their faces, "Here I am saying something clever and profound now" – and that is not from vanity, as it is with anyone like me, but one sees that she appreciates it awfully herself, and believes in it, and thinks a lot of it, and imagines that you think a lot of all that, just as she does. Oh, truthfulness! it's by that they conquer us. How exquisite it was in her!

I remember it, I have forgotten nothing! As soon as she had gone, I made up my mind. That same day I made my last investigations and found out every detail of her position at the moment; every detail of her past I had learned already from Lukerya, at that time a servant in the family, whom I had bribed a few days before. This position was so awful that I can't understand how she could laugh as she had done that day and feel interest in the words of Mephistopheles, when she was in such horrible straits. But — that's youth! That is just what I thought about her at the time with pride and joy; for, you know, there's a greatness of soul in it — to be able to say, "Though I am on the edge of the abyss, yet Goethe's grand words are radiant with light." Youth always has some greatness of soul, if its only a spark and that distorted. Though it's of her I am speaking, of her alone. And, above all, I looked upon her then as mine and did not doubt of my power. You know, that's a voluptuous idea when you feel no doubt of it.

But what is the matter with me? If I go on like this, when shall I put it all together and look at it as a whole. I must make haste, make haste — that is not what matters, oh, my God!

Chapter II

The offer of marriage

The "details" I learned about her I will tell in one word: her father and mother were dead, they had died three years before, and she had been left with two disreputable aunts: though it is saying too little to call them disreputable. One aunt was a widow with a large family (six children, one smaller than another), the other a horrid old maid. Both were horrid. Her father was in the service, but only as a copying clerk, and was only a gentleman by courtesy; in fact, everything was in my favor. I came as though from a higher world; I was anyway a retired lieutenant of a brilliant regiment, a gentleman by birth, independent and all the rest of it, and as for my pawnbroker's shop, her aunts could only have looked on that with respect. She had been living in slavery at her aunts' for those three years: yet she had managed to pass an examination somewhere — she managed to pass it, she wrung the time for it, weighed down as a she was by the pitiless burden of daily drudgery, and that proved something in the way of striving for what was higher and better on her part! Why, what made me want to marry her? Never mind me, though; of that later on . . . As though that mattered! — She taught her aunt's children; she made their clothes; and towards the end not only washed the clothes, but with her weak chest even scrubbed the floors. To put it plainly, they used to beat her, and taunt her with eating their bread. It ended by their scheming to sell her. Tfoo! I omit the filthy details. She told me all about it afterwards.

All this had been watched for a whole year by a neighbor, a fat shopkeeper, and not a humble one but the owner of two grocer's shops. He had ill-treated two wives and now he was looking for a third, and so he cast his eye on her. "She's a quiet one," he thought; "she's grown up in poverty, and I am marrying for the sake of my motherless children."

He really had children. He began trying to make the match and negotiating with the aunts. He was fifty years old, besides. She was aghast with horror. It was then she began coming so often to me to advertise in the Voice. At last she began begging the aunts to give her just a little time to think it over. They granted her that little time, but would not let her have more; they were always at her: "We don't know where to turn to find food for ourselves, without an extra mouth to feed."

I had found all this out already, and the same day, after what had happened in the morning, I made up my mind. That evening the shopkeeper came, bringing with him a pound of sweets from the shop; she was sitting with him, and I called Lukerya out of the kitchen and told her to go and whisper to her that I was at the gate and wanted to say something to her without delay. I felt pleased with myself. And altogether I felt awfully pleased all that day.

On the spot, at the gate, in the presence of Lukerya, before she had recovered from her amazement at my sending for her, I informed her that I should look upon it as an honor and happiness . . . telling her, in the next place, not to be surprised at the manner of my declaration and at my speaking at the gate, saying that I was a straightforward man and had learned the position of affairs. And I was not lying when I said I was straightforward. Well, hang it all. I did not only speak with propriety — that is, showing I was a man of decent breeding, but I spoke with originality and that was the chief thing. After all, is there any harm in admitting it? I want to judge myself and am judging myself. I must speak pro and contra, and I do. I remembered afterwards with enjoyment, though it was stupid, that I frankly declared, without the least embarrassment, that, in the first place, I was not particularly talented, not particularly intelligent, not particularly good-natured, rather a cheap egoist (I remember that expression, I thought of it on the way and was pleased with it) and that very probably there was a great deal that was disagreeable in me in other respects. All this was said with a special sort of pride — we all know how that sort of thing is said. Of course, I had good taste enough not to proceed to enlarge on my virtues after honorably enumerating my defects, not to say "to make up for that I have this and that and the other." I saw that she was still horribly frightened I purposely exaggerated. I told her straight out that she would have enough to eat, but that fine clothes, theaters, balls — she would have none of, at any rate not till later on, when I had attained my object. this severe tone was a positive delight to me. I added as cursorily as possible, that in adopting such a calling — that is, in keeping a pawnbroker's shop, I had one object, hinting there was a special circumstance . . . but I really had a right to say so: I really had such an aim and there really was such a circumstance. Wait a minute, gentlemen; I have always been the first to hate this pawn broking business, but in reality, though it is absurd to talk about oneself in such mysterious phrases, yet, you know, I was "revenging myself on society," I really was, I was, I was! So that her gibe that morning at the idea of my revenging myself was unjust. that is, do you see, if I had said to her straight out in words: "yes, I am revenging myself on society," she would have laughed as she did that morning, and it would, in fact have been absurd. But by indirect hints, but dropping mysterious phrases, it appeared that it was possible to work upon her imagination. Besides, I had no fears then: I knew that the fat shopkeeper was anyway more repulsive to her than I was, and that I, standing at the gate, had appeared as a deliverer. I understood that, of course. Oh, what is base a man understands particularly well! But was it base? How can a man judge? Didn't I love her even then?

Wait a bit: of course, I didn't breathe a word to her of doing her a benefit; the opposite, oh, quite the opposite; I made out that it was I that would be under an obligation to her, not she to me. Indeed, I said as much — I couldn't resist saying it — and it sounded stupid, perhaps, for I noticed a shade flit across her face. But altogether I won the day completely. Wait a bit, if I am to recall all that vileness, then I will tell of that worst beastliness. As I stood there what was stirring in my mind was, "You are tall, a good figure, educated and — speaking without conceit — good-looking." That is what was at work in my mind. I need hardly say that, on the spot, out there at the gate she said "yes." But . . . but I ought to add: that out there by the gate she thought a long time before she said "yes." She pondered for so long that I said to her, "Well?" — and could not even refrain from asking it with a certain swagger.

"Wait a little. I'm thinking."

And her little face was so serious, so serious that even then I might have read it! And I was mortified: "Can she be choosing between me and the grocer!" I thought. Oh, I did not understand then! I did not understand anything, anything, then! I did not understand till today! I remember Lukerya ran after me as I was going away, stopped me on the road and said, breathlessly: "God will reward you, sir, for taking our dear young lady; only don't speak of that to her — she's proud."

Proud, is she! "I like proud people," I thought. Proud people are particularly nice when . . . well, when one has no doubt of one's power over them, eh? Oh, base, tactless man! Oh, how pleased I was! You know, when she was standing there at the gate, hesitating whether to say "yes" to me, and I was wondering at it, you know, she may have had some such thought as this: "If it is to be misery either way, isn't it best to choose the very worst" — that is, let the fat grocer beat her to death when he was drunk! Eh! what do you think, could there have been a thought like that?

And, indeed, I don't understand it now, I don't understand it at all, even now. I have only just said that she may have had that thought: of two evils choose the worst — that is the grocer. But which was the worst for her then — the grocer or I? The grocer or the pawnbroker who quoted Goethe? That's another question! What a question! And even that you don't understand: the answer is lying on the table and you call it a question! Never mind me, though. It's not a question of me at all . . . and, by the way, what is there left for me now — whether it's a question of me or whether it is not? That's what I am utterly unable to answer. I had better go to bed. My head aches. . . .

Chapter III

The Noblest Of Men,
Though I don't believe it myself

I could not sleep. And how should I? There is a pulse throbbing in my head. One longs to master it all, all that degradation. Oh, the degradation! Oh, what degradation I dragged her out of then! Of course, she must have realized that, she must have appreciated my action! I was pleased, too, by various thoughts — for instance, the reflection that I was forty-one and she was only sixteen. that fascinated me, that feeling of inequality was very sweet, was very sweet.

I wanted, for instance, to have a wedding a l'anglaise, that is only the two of us, with just the two necessary witnesses, one of them Lukerya, and from the wedding straight to the train to Moscow (I happened to have business there, by the way), and then a fortnight at the hotel. She opposed it, she would not have it, and I had to visit her aunts and treat them with respect as though they were relations from whom I was taking her. I gave way, and all befitting respect was paid the aunts. I even made the creatures a present of a hundred rubles each and promised them more — not telling her anything about it, of course, that I might not make her feel humiliated by the lowness of her surroundings. the aunts were as soft as silk at once. There was a wrangle about the trousseau too; she had nothing, almost literally, but she did not want to have anything. I succeeded in proving to her, though, that she must have something, and I made up the trousseau, for who would have given her anything? But there, enough of me. I did, however, succeed in communicating some of my ideas to her then, so that she knew them anyway. I was in too great a hurry, perhaps. the best of it was that, from the very beginning, she rushed to meet me with love, greeted me with rapture, when I went to see her in the evening, told me in her chatter (the enchanting chatter of innocence) all about her childhood and girlhood, her old home, her father and mother. But I poured cold water upon all that at once. that was my idea. I met her enthusiasm with silence, friendly silence, of course . . . but, all the same, she could quickly see that we were different and that I was — an enigma. And being an enigma was what I made a point of most of all! Why, it was just for the sake of being an enigma, perhaps — that I have been guilty of all this stupidity. The first thing was sternness — it was with an air of sternness that I took her into my house. In fact, as I went about then feeling satisfied, I framed a complete system. Oh, it came of itself without any effort. And it could not have been otherwise. I was bound to create that system owing to one inevitable fact — why should I libel myself indeed! The system was a genuine one. yes, listen; if you must judge a man, better judge him knowing all about it . . . listen.

How am I to begin this, for it is very difficult. When

you begin to justify yourself — then it is difficult. You see, for instance, young people despise money — I made money of importance at once; I laid special stress on money. And laid such stress on it that she became more and more silent. She opened her eyes wide, listened, gazed and said nothing. you see, the young are heroic, that is the good among them are heroic and impulsive, but they have little tolerance; if the least thing is not quite right they are full of contempt. And I wanted breadth, I wanted to instill breadth into her very heart, to make it part of her inmost feeling, did I not? I'll take a trivial example: how should I explain my pawn-broker's shop to a character like that? Of course, I did not speak of it directly, or it would have appeared that I was apologizing, and I, so to speak, worked it through with pride, I almost spoke without words, and I am masterly at speaking without words. all my life I have spoken without words, and I have passed through whole tragedies on my own account without words. Why, I, too, have been unhappy! I was abandoned by everyone, abandoned and forgotten, and no one, no one knew it! And all at once this sixteen-year-old girl picked up details about me from vulgar people and thought she knew all about me, and, meanwhile, what was precious remained hidden in this heart! I went on being silent, with her especially I was silent, with her especially, right up to yesterday — why was I silent? Because I was proud. I wanted her to find out for herself, without my help, and not from the tales of low people; I wanted her to divine of herself what manner of man I was and to understand me! Taking her into my house I wanted all her respect, I wanted her to be standing before me in homage for the sake of my sufferings — and I deserved it. Oh, I have always been proud, I always wanted all or nothing! You see it was just because I am not one who will accept half a happiness, but always wanted all, that I was forced to act like that then: it was a much as to say, "See into me for yourself and appreciate me!" For you must see that if I had begun explaining myself to her and prompting her, ingratiating myself and asking for her respect — it would have been as good as asking for charity . . . But . . . but why am I talking of that!

Stupid, stupid, stupid, stupid! I explained to her than, in two words, directly, ruthlessly (and I emphasize the fact that it was ruthlessly) that the heroism of youth was charming, but — not worth a farthing. Why not? Because it costs them so little, because it is not gained through life; it is, so to say, merely "first impressions of existence," but just let us see you at work! Cheap heroism is always easy, and even to sacrifice life is easy too; because it is only a case of hot blood and an overflow of energy, and there is such a longing for what is beautiful! No, take the deed of heroism that is laborious, obscure, without noise or flourish, slandered, in which there is a great deal of sacrifice and not one grain of glory — in which you, a splendid man, are made to look like a scoundrel before everyone, though you might be the most honest man in the world — you try that sort of heroism and you'll soon give it up! While I — have been bearing the burden of that all my life. At first she argued — oh, how she argued — but afterwards she began to be silent, completely silent, in fact, only opened her eyes wide as she listened, such big, big eyes, so attentive. And . . . and what is more, I suddenly saw a smile, mistrustful, silent, an evil smile. Well, it was with that smile on her face I brought her into my house. It is true that she had nowhere to go.

Chapter IV

Plans and Plans

Which of us began it first?
Neither. It began of itself from the very first. I have said that with sternness I brought her into the house. From the first step, however, I softened it. Before she was married it was explained to her that she would have to take pledges and pay out money, and she said nothing at the time (note that). What is more, she set to work with positive zeal. Well, of course, my lodging, my furniture all remained as before. My lodging consisted of two rooms, a large room from which the shop was partitioned off, and a second one, also large, our living room and bedroom. My furniture is scanty: even her aunts had better things. My shrine of icons with the lamp was in the outer room where the shop is; in the inner room my bookcase with a few books in and a trunk of which I keep the key; married I told her that one ruble a day and not more, was to be spent on our board — that is, on food for me, her and Lukerya whom

I had enticed to come to us. "I must have thirty thousand in three years," said I, "and we can't save the money if we spend more." She fell in with this, but I raised the sum by thirty kopecks a day. It was the same with the theater. I told her before marriage that she would not go to the theater, and yet I decided once a month to go to he theater, and in a decent way, to the stalls. We went together. We went three times and saw The Hunt after Happiness, and Singing Birds, I believe. (Oh, what does it matter!) We went in silence and in silence we returned. Why, why, from the very beginning, did we take to being silent? From the very first, you know, we had no quarrels, but always the same silence. She was always, I remember, watching me stealthily in those days; as soon as I noticed it I became more silent that before. It is true that it was I insisted on the silence, not she. On her part there were one or two outbursts, she rushed to embrace me; but as these outbursts were hysterical, painful, and I wanted secure happiness, with respect from her, I received them coldly. And indeed, I was right; each time the outburst was followed next day by a quarrel.

Though, again, there were no quarrels, but there was silence and — and on her side a more and more defiant air. "Rebellion and independence," that's what it was, only she didn't know how to show it. yes, that gentle creature was becoming more and more defiant. Would you believe it, I was becoming revolting to her? I learned that. And there could be no doubt that she was moved to frenzy at times. think, for instance, of her beginning to sniff at our poverty, after her coming from such sordidness and destitution — from scrubbing the floors! you see, there was no poverty; there was frugality, but there was abundance of what was necessary, of linen, for instance, and the greatest cleanliness. I always used to dream that cleanliness in a husband attracts a wife. It was not our poverty she was scornful of, but my supposed miserliness in the housekeeping: "he has his objects," she seemed to say, "he is showing his strength of will." She suddenly refused to go to the theater. And more and more often an ironical look. . . . And I was more silent, more and more silent.

I could not begin justifying myself, could I? What was at the bottom of all this was the pawn broking business. Allow me, I knew that a woman, above all at sixteen, must be in complete subordination to a man. Women have no originality. That — that is an axiom; even now, even now, for me it is an axiom! What does it prove that she is lying there in the outer room? Truth is truth, and even Mill is no use against it! And a woman who loves, oh, a woman who loves idealizes even the vices, even the villainies of the man she loves. He would not himself even succeed in finding such justification for his villainies as she will find for him. that is generous but not original. it is the lack of originality alone that has been the ruin of women. and, I repeat, what is the use of your point to that table? Why, what is there original in her being on that table? O – O – Oh!

Listen. I was convinced of her love at that time. Why, she used to throw herself on my neck in those days. She loved me; that is, more accurately, she wanted to love. Yes, that's just what it was, she wanted to love; she was trying to love. And the point was that in this case there were no villainies for which she had to find justification. you will say, I'm a pawnbroker; and everyone says the same. But what if I am a pawnbroker? It follows that there must be reasons since the most generous of men had become a pawnbroker. You see, gentlemen, there are ideas . . . that is, if one expresses some ideas, utters them in words, the effect is very stupid. The effect is to make one ashamed. For what reason? For no reason. Because we are all wretched creatures and cannot hear the truth, or I do not know why. I said just now, "the most generous of men" — that is absurd, and yet that is how it was. It's the truth, that is, the absolute, absolute truth! Yes, I had the right to want to make myself secure and open that pawnbroker's shop: "You have rejected me, you — people, I mean — you have cast me out with contemptuous silence. My passionate yearning towards you you have met with insult all my life. Now I have the right to put up a wall against you, to save up that thirty thousand rubles and end my life somewhere in the Crimea, on the south coast, among the mountains and vineyards, on my own estate bought with that thirty thousand, and above everything, far away from you all, living without malice against you, with an ideal in my soul, with a beloved woman at my heart, and a family, if God sends one, and — helping the inhabitants all around."

Of course, it is quite right that I say this to myself now, but what could have been more stupid than describing all that aloud to her? That was the cause of my proud silence, that's why we sat in silence. For what could she have understood? Sixteen years old, the earliest youth — yes, what could she have understood of my justification, of my sufferings? Undeviating straightness, ignorance of life, the cheap convictions of youth, the henlike blindness of those "noble hearts," and what stood for most was — the pawnbroker's shop and — enough! (And was I a villain in the pawnbroker's shop? Did not she see how I acted? Did I extort too much?)

Oh, how awful is truth on earth! That exquisite creature, that gentle spirit, that heaven — she was a tyrant, she was the insufferable tyrant and torture of my soul! I should be unfair to myself if I didn't say so! You imagine I didn't love her? Who can say that I did not love her! Do you see, it was a case of irony, the malignant irony of fate and nature! We were under a curse, the life of men in general is under a curse! (mine in particular). Of course, I understand now that I made some mistake! Something went wrong. Everything was clear, my plan was clear as daylight: "Austere and proud, asking for no moral comfort, but suffering in silence." And that was how it was. I was not lying, I was not lying! "She will see for herself, later on, that it was heroic, only that she had not known how to see it, and when, some day, she divines, it she will prize me ten times more and will abase herself in the dust and fold her hands in homage" — that was my plan. But I forgot something or lost sight of it. There was something I failed to manage. But, enough, enough! And whose forgiveness am I to ask now? What is done is done. By bolder, man, and have some pride! It is not your fault. . . !

Well, I will tell the truth, I am not afraid to face the truth; it was her fault, her fault!

Chapter V

A Gentle Spirit in Revolt

Quarrels began from her suddenly beginning to pay out loans on her own account, to price things above their worth, and even, on two occasions, she deigned to enter into a dispute about it with me. I did not agree. But then the captain's widow turned up.

This old widow brought a medallion — a present from her dead husband, a souvenir, of course. I lent her thirty rubles on it. She fell to complaining, begged me to keep the thing for her — of course we do keep things. Well, in short, she came again to exchange it for a bracelet that was not worth eight rubles; I, of course, refused. She must have guessed something from my wife's eyes, anyway she came again when I was not there and my wife changed it for the medallion.

Discovering it the same day, I spoke mildly but firmly and reasonably. She was sitting on the bed, looking at the ground and tapping with her right foot on the carpet (her characteristic movement); there was an ugly smile on her lips. Then, without raising my voice in the least, I explained calmly that the money was mine, that I had a right to look at life with my own eyes and — and that when I had offered to take her into my house, I had hidden nothing from her.

She suddenly leapt up, suddenly began shaking all over and — what do you think — she suddenly stamped her foot at me; it was a wild animal, it was a frenzy, it was the frenzy of a wild animal. I was petrified with astonishment; I had never expected such an outburst. But I did not lose my head. I made no movement even, and again, in the same calm voice, I announced plainly that from that time forth I should deprive her of the part she took in my work. She laughed in my face, and walked out of the house.

The fact is, she had not the right to walk out of the house. Nowhere without me, such was the agreement before she was married. In the evening she returned; I did not utter a word.

The next day, too, she went out in the morning, and the day after again. I shut the shop and went off to her aunts. I had cut off all relations with them from the time of the wedding — I would not have them to see me, and I would not go to see them. But it turned out that she had not been with them. They listened to me with curiosity and laughed in my face: "It serves you right," they said. But I expected their laughter. At that point, then I bought over the younger aunt, the unmarried one, for a hundred rubles, giving her twenty-five in advance. Two days later she came to me: "There's an officer called Efimovitch mixed up in this," she said; "a lieutenant who was a comrade of yours in the regiment."

I was greatly amazed. That Efimovitch had done me more harm than anyone in the regiment, and about a month ago, being a shameless fellow, he once or twice came into the shop with a pretence of pawning something, and I remember, began laughing with my wife. I went up at the time and told him not to dare to come to me, recalling our relations; but there was no thought of anything in my head, I simply thought that he was insolent. Now the aunt suddenly informed me that she had already appointed to see him and that the whole business had been arranged by a former friend of the aunt's, the widow of a colonel, called Yulia Samsonovna. "It's to her," she said, "your wife goes now."

I will cut the story short. The business cost me three hundred rubles, but in a couple of days it had been arranged that I should stand in an adjoining room, behind closed doors, and listen to the first rendezvous between my wife and Efimovitch, tête-à-tête. Meanwhile, the evening before, a scene, brief but very memorable for me, took place between us.

She returned towards evening, sat down on the bed, looked at me sarcastically, and tapped on the carpet with her foot. Looking at her, the idea suddenly came into my mind that for the whole of the last month, or rather, the last fortnight, her character had not been her own; one might even say that it had been the opposite of her own; she had suddenly shown herself a mutinous, aggressive creature; I cannot say shameless, but regardless of decorum and eager for trouble. She went out of her way to stir up trouble. Her gentleness hindered her, though. When a girl like that rebels, however outrageously she may behave, one can always see that she is forcing herself to do it, that she is driving herself to do it, and that it is impossible for her to master and overcome her own modesty and shamefacedness. That is why such people go such lengths at times, so that one can hardly believe one's eyes. One who is accustomed to depravity, on the contrary, always softens things, acts more disgustingly, but with a show of decorum and seemliness by which she claims to be superior to you.

"Is it true that you were turned out of the regiment because you were afraid to fight a duel?" she asked suddenly, apropos of nothing — and her eyes flashed.

"It is true that by the sentence of the officers I was asked to give up my commission, though, as a fact, I had sent in my papers before that."

"You were turned out as a coward?"

"Yes, they sentenced me as a coward. But I refused to fight a duel, not from cowardice, but because I would not submit to their tyrannical decision and send a challenge when I did not consider myself insulted. You know," I could not refrain from adding, "that to resist such tyranny and to accept the consequences meant showing far more manliness than fighting any kind of duel."

I could not resist it. I dropped the phrase, as it were, in self-defense, and that was all she wanted, this fresh humiliation for me.

She laughed maliciously.

"And is it true that for three years afterwards you wandered about the streets of Petersburg like a tramp, begging for coppers and spending your nights in billiard-rooms?"

"I even spent the night in Vyazemsky's House in the Haymarket. Yes, it is true; there was much disgrace and degradation in my life after I left the regiment, but not moral degradation, because even at the time I hated what I did more than anyone. It was only the degradation of my will and my mind, and it was only caused by the desperateness of my position. But that is over...."

"Oh, now you are a personage — a financier!"

A hint at the pawnbroker's shop. But by then I had succeeded in recovering my mastery of myself. I saw that she was thirsting for explanations that be humiliating to me and — I did not give them. A customer rang the bell very opportunely, and I went out into the shop. An hour later, when she was dressed to go out, she stood still, facing me, and said —

"You didn't tell me anything about that, though, before our marriage?"

I made no answer and she went away.

And so next day I was standing in that room, the other side of the door, listening to hear how my fate was being decided, and in my pocket I had a revolver. She was dressed better than usual and sitting at a the table, and Efimovitch was showing off before her. And after all, it turned out exactly (I say it to my credit) as I had foreseen and had assumed it would, though I was not conscious of having foreseen and assumed it. I do not know whether I express myself intelligibly.

This is what happened.

I listened for a whole hour. For a whole hour I was present at a duel between a noble, lofty woman and a worldly, corrupt, dense man with a crawling soul. And how, I wondered in amazement, how could that naïve, gentle, silent girl have come to know all that? The wittiest author of a society comedy could not have created such a scene of mockery, of naïve laughter, and of the holy contempt of virtue for vice. And how brilliant her sayings, her little phrases were: what wit there was in her rapid answers, what truths in her condemnation. And, at the same time, what almost girlish simplicity. She laughed in his face at his declarations of love, at his gestures, at his proposals. Coming coarsely to the point at once, and not expecting to meet with opposition, he was utterly nonplussed. At first I might have imagined that it was simply coquetry on her part — "the coquetry of a witty, though depraved creature to enhance her own value." But no, the truth shone out like the sun, and to doubt was impossible. It was only an exaggerated and impulsive hatred for me that had led her, in her inexperience, to arrange this interview, but, when it came off — her eyes were opened at once. She was simply in desperate haste to mortify me, come what might, but though she had brought herself to do something so low she could not endure unseemliness. And could she, so pure and sinless, with an ideal in her heart, have been seduced by Efimovitch or any worthless snob? On the contrary, she was only moved to laughter by him. All her goodness rose up from her soul and her indignation roused her to sarcasm. I repeat, the buffoon was completely nonplussed at last and sat frowning, scarcely answering, so much so that I began to be afraid that he might insult her, from a mean desire for revenge. And I repeat again: to my credit, I listened to that scene almost without surprise. I met, as it were, nothing but what I knew well. I had gone, as it were, on purpose to meet it, believing not a word of it, not a word said against her, though I did take the revolver in my pocket — that is the truth. And could I have imagined her different? For what did I love her, for what did I prize her, for what had I married her? Oh, of course, I was quite convinced of her hate for me, but at the same time I was quite convinced of her sinlessness. I suddenly cut short the scene by opening the door. Efimovitch leapt up. I took her by the hand and suggested she should go home with me. Efimovitch recovered himself and suddenly burst into loud peals of laughter.

"Oh, to sacred conjugal rights I offer no opposition; take her away, take her away! And you know," he shouted after me, "though no decent man could fight you, yet from respect to your lady I am at your service . . . If you are ready to risk yourself."

"Do you hear?" I said, stopping her for a second in

the doorway.

After which not a word was said all the way home. I led her by the arm and she did not resist. On the contrary, she was greatly impressed, and this lasted after she got home. On reaching home she sat down in a chair and fixed her eyes upon me. She was extremely pale; though her lips were compressed ironically yet she looked at me with solemn and austere defiance and seemed convinced in earnest, for the minute, that I should kill her with the revolver. But I took the revolver from my pocket without a word and laid it on the table! She looked at me and at the revolver (note that the revolver was already an object familiar to her. I had kept one loaded ever since I opened the shop. I made up my mind when I set up the shop that I would not keep a huge dog or a strong manservant, as Mozer does, for instance. My cook opens the doors to my visitors. But in our trade it is impossible to be without means of self-defense in case of emergency, and I kept a loaded revolver. In early days, when first she was living in my house, she took great interest in that revolver, and asked questions about it, and I even explained its construction and working; I even persuaded her once to fire at a target. Note all that). Taking no notice of her frightened eyes, I lay down on the bed, half-undressed. I felt very much exhausted; it was by then about eleven o'clock. She went on sitting in the same place, not stirring, for another hour. Then she put out the candle and she, too, without undressing, lay down on the sofa near the wall. For the first time she did not sleep with me — note that too. . . .

Chapter VI

A Terrible Reminiscence

Now for a terrible reminiscence....

I woke up, I believe, before eight o'clock, and it was very nearly broad daylight. I woke up completely to full consciousness and opened my eyes. She was standing at the table holding the revolver in her hand. She did not see that I had woken up and was looking at her. And suddenly I saw that she had begun moving towards me with the revolver in her hand. I quickly closed my eyes and pretended to be still asleep.

She came up to the bed and stood over me. I heard everything; though a dead silence had fallen I heard that silence. All at once there was a convulsive movement and, irresistibly, against my will, I suddenly opened my eyes. She was looking straight at me, straight into my eyes, and the revolver was at my temple. Our eyes met. But we looked at each other for no more than a moment. With an effort I shut my eyes again, and at the same instant I resolved that I would not stir and would not open my eyes, whatever might be awaiting me.

It does sometimes happen that people who are sound asleep suddenly open their eyes, even raise their heads for a second and look about the room, then, a moment later, they lay their heads again on the pillow unconscious, and fall asleep without understanding anything. When meeting her eyes and feeling the revolver on my forehead, I closed my eyes and remained motionless, as though in a deep sleep — she certainly might have supposed that I really was asleep, and that I had seen nothing, especially as it was utterly improbable that, after seeing what I had seen, I should shut my eyes again at such a moment.

Yes, it was improbable. But she might guess the truth all the same — that thought flashed upon my mind at once, all at the same instant. Oh, what a whirl of thoughts and sensations rushed into my mind in less than a minute. Hurrah for the electric speed of thought! In that case (so I felt), if she guessed the truth and knew that I was awake, I should crush her by my readiness to accept death, and her hand might tremble. Her determination might be shaken by a new, overwhelming impression. They say that people standing on a height have an impulse to throw themselves down. I imagine that many suicides and murders have been committed simply because the revolver has been in the hand. It is like a precipice, with an incline of an angle of forty-five degrees, down which you cannot help sliding, and something impels you irresistibly to pull the trigger. But the knowledge that I had seen, that I knew it all, and was waiting for death at her hands without a word — might hold her back on the incline.

The stillness was prolonged, and all at once I felt on my temple, on my hair, the cold contact of iron. You will ask: did I confidently expect to escape? I will answer you as God is my judge: I had no hope of it, except one chance in a hundred. Why did I accept death? But I will ask, what use was life to me after that revolver had been raised against me by the being I adored? Besides, I knew with the whole strength of my being that there was a struggle going on between us, a fearful duel for life and death, the duel fought be the coward of yesterday, rejected by his comrades for cowardice. I knew that and she knew it, if only she guessed the truth that I was not asleep.

Perhaps that was not so, perhaps I did not think that then, but yet it must have been so, even without conscious thought, because I've done nothing but think of it every hour of my life since.

But you will ask me again: why did you not save her from such wickedness? Oh! I've asked myself that question a thousand times since — every time that, with a shiver down my back, I recall that second. But at that moment my soul was plunged in dark despair! I was lost, I myself was lost — how could I save anyone? And how do you know whether I wanted to save anyone then? How can one tell what I could be feeling then?

My mind was in a ferment, though; the seconds passed; she still stood over me — and suddenly I shuddered with hope! I quickly opened my eyes. She was no longer in the room: I got out of bed: I had conquered — and she was conquered forever!

I went to the samovar. We always had the samovar brought into the outer room and she always poured out the tea. I sat down at the table without a word and took a glass of tea from her. Five minutes later I looked at her. She was fearfully pale, even paler than the day before, and she looked at me. And suddenly . . . and suddenly, seeing that I was looking at her, she gave a pale smile with her pale lips, with a timid question in her eyes. "So she still doubts and is asking herself: does he know or doesn't he know; did he see or didn't he?" I turned my eyes away indifferently. After tea I close the shop, went to the market and bought an iron bedstead and a screen. Returning home, I directed that the bed should be put in the front room and shut off with a screen. It was a bed for her, but I did not say a word to her. She understood without words, through that bedstead, that I "had seen and knew all," and that all doubt was over. At night I left the revolver on the table, as I always did. At night she got into her new bed without a word: our marriage bond was broken, "she was conquered but not forgiven." At night she began to be delirious, and in the morning she had brain-fever. She was in bed for six weeks.

Part II

Chapter I

The Dream of Pride

*L*ukerya has just announced that she can't go on living here and that she is going away as soon as her lady is buried. I knelt down and prayed for five minutes. I wanted to pray for an hour, but I keep thinking and thinking, and always sick thoughts, and my head aches — what is the use of praying? — it's only a sin! It is strange, too, that I am not sleepy: in great, too great sorrow, after the first outbursts one is always sleepy. Men condemned to death, they say, sleep very soundly on the last night. And so it must be, it is the law of nature, otherwise their strength would not hold out . . . I lay down on the sofa but I did not sleep. . . .

... For the six weeks of her illness we were looking after her day and night — Lukerya and I together with a trained nurse whom I had engaged from the hospital. I spared no expense — in fact, I was eager to spend my money for her. I called in Dr. Shreder and paid him ten rubles a visit. When she began to get better I did not show myself so much. But why am I describing it? When she got up again, she sat quietly and silently in my room at a special table, which I had bought for her, too, about that time. . . . Yes, that's the truth, we were absolutely silent; that is, we began talking afterwards, but only of the daily routine. I purposely avoided expressing myself, but I noticed that she, too, was glad not to have to say a word more than was necessary. It seemed to me that this was perfectly normal on her part: "She is too much shattered, too completely conquered," I thought, "and I must let her forget and grow used to it." In this way we were silent, but every minute I was preparing myself for the future. I thought that she was too, and it was fearfully interesting to me to guess what she was thinking about to herself then.

I will say more: oh! of course, no one knows what I went through, moaning over her in her illness. But I stifled my moans in my own heart, even from Lukerya. I could not imagine, could not even conceive of her dying without knowing the whole truth. When she was out of danger and began to regain her health, I very quickly and completely, I remember, recovered my tranquility. What is more, I made up my mind to defer out future as long as possible, and meanwhile to leave things just as they were. Yes, something strange and peculiar happened to me then, I cannot call it anything else: I had triumphed, and the mere consciousness of that was enough for me. So the whole winter passes. Oh! I was satisfied as I had never been before, and it lasted the whole winter.

You see, there had been a terrible external circumstance in my life which, up till then — that is, up to the catastrophe with my wife — had weighed upon me everyday and every hour. I mean the loss of my reputation and my leaving the regiment. In two words, I was treated with tyrannical injustice. It is true my comrades did not love me because of my difficult character, and perhaps because of my absurd character, though it often happens that what is exalted, precious and of value to one, for some reason amuses the herd of one's companions. Oh, I was never liked, not even at school! I was always and everywhere disliked. Even Lukerya cannot like me. What happened in the regiment, though it was the result of their dislike to me, was in a sense accidental. I mention this because nothing is more mortifying and insufferable than to be ruined by an accident, which might have happened or not have happened, from an unfortunate accumulation of circumstances which might have passed over like a cloud. For an intelligent being it is humiliating. This is what happened.

In an interval, at a theater, I went out to the refreshment bar. A hussar called A—— came in and began, before all the officers present and the public, loudly talking to two other hussars, telling them that Captain Bezumtsev, of our regiment, was making a disgraceful scene in the passage and was, "he believed, drunk." The conversation did not go further and, indeed, it was a mistake, for Captain Bezumtsev was not drunk and the "disgraceful scene" was not really disgraceful. The hussars began talking of something else, and the matter ended there, but the next day the story reached our regiment, and then they began saying at once that I was the only officer of our regiment in the refreshment bar at the time, and that when A—— the hussar, had spoken insolently of Captain Bezumtsev, I had not gone up to A—— and stopped him by remonstrating. But on what grounds could I have done so? If he had a grudge against Bezumtsev, it was their personal affair and why should I interfere? Meanwhile, the officers began to declare that it was not a personal affair, but that it concerned the regiment, and as I was the only officer of the regiment present I had thereby shown all the officers and other people in the refreshment bar that there could be officers in our regiment who were not oversensitive on the score of their own honor and the honor of their regiment. I could not agree with this view. they let me know that I could set everything right if I were willing, even now, late as it was, to demand a formal explanation from A——. I was not willing to do this, and as I was irritated I refused with pride. And thereupon I forthwith resigned my commission — that is the whole story. I left the regiment, proud but crushed in spirit. I was depressed in will and mind. Just then it was that my sister's husband in Moscow squandered all our little property and my portion of it, which was tiny enough, but the loss of it left me homeless, without a farthing. I might have taken a job in a private business, but I did not. After wearing a distinguished uniform I could not take work in a railway office. And so — if it must be shame, let it be shame; if it must be disgrace, let it be disgrace; if it must be degradation, let it be degradation — (the worse it is, the better) that was my choice. Then followed three years of gloomy memories, and even Vyazemsky's House. A year and a half ago my godmother, a wealthy old lady, died in Moscow, and to my surprise left me three thousand in her will. I thought a little and immediately decided on my course of action. I determined on setting up as a pawnbroker, without apologizing to anyone: money, then a home, as far as possible from memories of the past, that was my plan. Nevertheless, the gloomy past and my ruined reputation fretted me everyday, every hour. But then I married. Whether it was by chance or not I don't know. but when I brought her into my home I thought I was bringing a friend, and I needed a friend so much. But I saw clearly that the friend must be trained, schooled, even conquered. Could I have explained myself straight off to a girl of sixteen with her prejudices? How, for instance, could I, without the chance help of the horrible incident with the revolver, have made her believe I was not a coward, and that I had been unjustly accused of cowardice in the regiment? But that terrible incident came just in the nick of time. Standing the test of the revolver, I scored off all my gloomy past. And though no one knew about it, she knew, and for me that was everything, because she was everything for me, all the hope of the future that I cherished in my dreams! She was the one person I had prepared for myself, and I needed no one else — and here she knew everything; she knew, at any rate, that she had been in haste to join my enemies against me unjustly. That thought enchanted me. In her eyes I could not be a scoundrel now, but at most a strange person, and that thought after all that had happened was by no means displeasing to me; strangeness is not a vice — on the contrary, it sometimes attracts the feminine heart. In fact, I purposely deferred the climax: what had happened was meanwhile, enough for my peace of mind and provided a great number of pictures and materials for my dreams. That is what is wrong, that I am a dreamer: I had enough material for my dreams, and about her, I thought she could wait.

So the whole winter passed in a sort of expectation. I liked looking at her on the sly, when she was sitting at her little table. She was busy at her needlework, and sometimes in the evening she read books taken from my bookcase. The choice of books in the bookcase must have had an influence in my favor too. She hardly ever went out. Just before dusk, after dinner, I used to take her out everyday for a walk. We took a constitutional, but we were not absolutely silent, as we used to be. I tried, in fact, to make a show of our not being silent, but talking harmoniously, but as I have said already, we both avoided letting ourselves go. I did it purposely, I thought it was essential to "give her time." Of course, it was strange that almost till the end of the winter it did not once strike me that, though I love to watch her stealthily, I had never once, all the winter, caught her glancing at me! I thought it was timidity in her. Besides, she had an air of such timid gentleness, such weakness after her illness. Yes, better to wait and — "she will come to you all at once of herself. . . ."

That thought fascinated me beyond all words. I will add one thing; sometimes, as it were purposely, I worked myself up and brought my mind and spirit to the point of believing she had injured me. And so it went on for some time. But my anger could never be very real or violent. And I felt myself as though it were only acting. And though I had broken off out marriage by buying that bedstead and screen, I could never, never look upon her as a criminal. And not that I took a frivolous view of her crime, but because I had the sense to forgive her completely, from the very first day, even before I bought the bedstead. In fact, it is strange on my part, for I am strict in moral questions. On the contrary, in my eyes, she was so conquered, so humiliated, so crushed, that sometimes I felt agonies of pity for her, though sometimes the thought of her humiliation was actually pleasing to me. The thought of our inequality pleased me. . . .

I intentionally performed several acts of kindness that winter. I excused two debts, I have one poor woman money without any pledge. And I said nothing to my wife about it, and I didn't do it in order that she should know; but the woman came to thank me, almost on her knees. And in that way it became public property; it seemed to me that she heard about the woman with pleasure.

But spring was coming, it was mid-April, we took out the double windows and the sun began lighting up our silent room with its bright beams. but there was, as it were, a veil before my eyes and a blindness over my mind. A fatal, terrible veil! How did it happen that the scales suddenly fell from my eyes, and I suddenly saw and understood? Was it a chance, or had the hour come, or did the ray of sunshine kindle a thought, a conjecture, in my dull mind? No, it was not a thought, not a conjecture. But a chord suddenly vibrated, a feeling that had long been dead was stirred and came to life, flooding all my darkened soul and devilish pride with light. It was as though I had suddenly leaped up from my place. And, indeed, it happened suddenly and abruptly. It happened towards evening, at five o'clock, after dinner. . . .

Chapter II

The Veil Suddenly Falls

*T*wo words first. A month ago I noticed a strange melancholy in her, not simply silence, but melancholy. That, too, I noticed suddenly. She was sitting at her work, her head bent over her sewing, and she did not see that I was looking at her. And it suddenly struck me that she had grown so delicate-looking, so thin, that her face was pale, her lips were white. All this, together with her melancholy, struck me all at once. I had already heard a little dry cough, especially at night. I got up at once and went off to ask Shreder to come, saying nothing to her.

Shreder came next day. She was very much surprised and looked first at Shreder and then at me.

"But I am well," she said, with an uncertain smile.

Shreder did not examine her very carefully (these doctors are sometimes superciliously careless), he only said to me in the other room, that it was just the result of her illness, and that it wouldn't be amiss to go for a trip to the sea in the spring, or, if that were impossible to take a cottage out of town for the summer. In fact, he said nothing except that there was weakness, or something of that sort. When Shreder had gone, she said again, looking at me very earnestly —

"I am quite well, quite well."

But as she said this she suddenly flushed, apparently from shame. Apparently it was shame. Oh! now I understand: she was ashamed that I was still her husband, that I was looking after her still as though I were a real husband. But at the time I did not understand and put down her blush to humility (the veil!).

And so, a month later, in April, at five o'clock on a bright sunny day, I was sitting in the shop making up my accounts. Suddenly I heard her, sitting in our room, at work at her table, begin softly, softly . . . singing. This novelty made an overwhelming impression upon me, and to this day I don't understand it. Till then I had hardly ever heard her sing, unless, perhaps, in those first days, when we were still able to be playful and practice shooting at a target. Then her voice was rather strong, resonant; though not quit true it was very sweet and healthy. now her little song was so faint — it was not that it was melancholy (it was some sort of ballad), but in her voice there was something jangled, broken, as though her voice were not equal to it, as though the song itself were sick. She sang in an undertone, and suddenly, as her voice rose, it broke — such a poor little voice, it broke so pitifully; she cleared her throat and again began softly, softly singing. . . .

My emotions will be ridiculed, but no one will understand why I was so moved! No, I was still not sorry for her, it was still something quite different. At the beginning, for the first minute, at any rate, I was filled with sudden perplexity and terrible amazement — a terrible and strange, painful and almost vindictive amazement: "She is singing, and before me; has she forgotten about me?"

Completely overwhelmed, I remained where I was, then I suddenly got up, took my hat and went out, as it were, without thinking. At least I don't know why or where I was going. Lukerya began giving me my overcoat.

"She is singing?" I said to Lukerya involuntarily. She did not understand, and looked at me still without understanding; and, indeed, I was really unintelligible.

"Is it the first time she is singing?"

"No, she sometimes does sing when you are out," answered Lukerya.

I remember everything. I went downstairs, went out into the street and walked along at random. I walked to the corner and began looking into the distance. People were passing by, the pushed against me. I did not feel it. I called a cab and told the man, I don't know why, to drive to Politseysky Bridge. Then suddenly changed my mind and gave him twenty kopecks.

"That's for my having troubled you," I said, with a meaningless laugh, but a sort of ecstasy was suddenly shining within me.

I returned home, quickening my steps. The poor little jangled, broken note was ringing in my heart again. My breath failed me. The veil was falling, was falling from my eyes! Since she sang before me, she had forgotten me — that is what was clear and terrible. My heart felt it. But rapture was glowing in my soul and it overcame my terror.

Oh! the irony of fate! Why, there had been nothing else, and could have been nothing else but that rapture in my soul all the winter, but where had I been myself all the winter? Had I been there together with my soul? I ran up the stairs in great haste, I don't know whether I went in timidly. I only remember that the whole floor seemed to be rocking and I felt as though I were floating on a river. I went into the room. She was sitting in the same place as before, with her head cursorily and without interest at me; it was hardly a look but just a habitual and indifferent movement upon somebody's coming into the room.

I went straight up and sat down beside her in a chair abruptly, as though I were mad. She looked at me quickly, seeming frightened; I took her hand and I don't remember what I said to her — that is, tried to say, for I could not even speak properly. My voice broke and would not obey me and I did not know what to say. I could only gasp for breath.

"Let us talk . . . you know . . . tell me something!" I muttered something stupid. Oh! how could I help being stupid? She started again and drew back in great alarm, looking at my face, but suddenly there was an expression of stern surprise in her eyes. Yes, surprise and stern. She looked at me with wide-open eyes. That sternness, that stern surprise shattered me at once: "So you still expect love? Love?" that surprise seemed to be asking, though she said nothing. But I read it all, I read it all. Everything within me seemed quivering, and I simply fell down at her feet. Yes, I groveled at her feet. She jumped up quickly, but I held her forcibly by both hands.

And I fully understood my despair — I understood it! But, would you believe it? ecstasy was surging up in my head so violently that I thought I should die. I kissed her feet in delirium and rapture. Yes, in immense, infinite rapture, and that, in spite of understanding all the hopelessness of my despair. I wept, said something, but could not speak. Her alarm and amazement were followed by some uneasy misgiving, some grave question, and she looked at me strangely, wildly even; she wanted to understand something quickly and she smiled. She was horribly ashamed at my kissing her feet and she drew them back. But I kissed the place on the floor where her foot had rested. She saw it and suddenly began laughing with shame (you know how it is when people laugh with shame). She became hysterical, I saw that her hands trembled — I did not think about that but went on muttering that I loved her, that I would not get up. "Let me kiss your dress . . . and worship you like this all my life." . . . I don't know, I don't remember — but suddenly she broke into sobs and trembled all over. A terrible fit of hysterics followed. I had frightened her.

I carried her to the bed. When the attack had passed off, sitting on the edge of the bed, with a terribly exhausted look, she took my two hands and begged me to calm myself: "Come, come, don't distress yourself, be calm!" and she began crying again. All that evening I did not leave her side. I kept telling her I should take her to Boulogne to bathe in the sea now, at once, in a fortnight, that she had such a broken voice, I had heard it that afternoon, that I would shut up the shop, that I would sell it Dobronravov, that everything should begin afresh and, above all, Boulogne, Boulogne! She listened and was still afraid. She grew more and more afraid. But that was not what mattered most for me: what mattered most to me was the more and more irresistible longing to fall at her feet again, and again to kiss and kiss the spot where her foot had rested, and to worship her; and — "I ask nothing, nothing more of you," I kept repeating, "do not answer me, take no notice of me, only let me watch you from my corner, treat me as your dog, your thing. . . ." She was crying.

"I thought you would let me go on like that," suddenly broke from her unconsciously, so unconsciously that, perhaps, she did not notice what she had said, and yet — oh, that was the most significant, momentous phrase she uttered that evening, the easiest for me to understand, and it stabbed my heart as though with a knife! It explained everything to me, everything, but while she was beside me, before my eyes, I could not help hoping and was fearfully happy. Oh, I exhausted her fearfully that evening. I understood that, but I kept thinking that I should alter everything directly. At last, towards night, she utterly exhausted. I persuaded her to go to sleep and she fell sound asleep at once. I expected her to be delirious, she was a little delirious, but very slightly. I kept getting up every minute in the night and going softly in my slippers to look at her. I wrung my hands over her, looking at that frail creature in that wretched little iron bedstead which I had bought for three rubles. I knelt down, but did not dare to kiss her feet in her sleep (without her consent). I began praying but leapt up again. Lukerya kept watch over me and came in and out from the kitchen. I went in to her, and told her to go to bed, and that tomorrow "things would be quite different."

And I believed in this, blindly, madly.

Oh, I was brimming over with rapture, rapture! I was eager for the next day. Above all, I did not believe that anything could go wrong, in spite of the symptoms. Reason had not altogether come back to me, though the veil had fallen from my eyes, and for a long, long time it did not come back — not till today, not till this very day! Yes, and how could it have come back then: why, she was still alive then; why, she was here before my eyes, and I was before her eyes: "Tomorrow she will wake up and I will tell her all this, and she will see it all." That was how I reasoned then, simply and clearly, because I was in an ecstasy! My great idea was the trip to Boulogne. I kept thinking for some reason that Boulogne would be everything, that there was something final and decisive about Boulogne. "To Boulogne, to Boulogne!" . . . I waited frantically for the morning.

Chapter III
I Understand Too Well

But you know that was only a few days ago, five days, only five days ago, last Tuesday! Yes, yes, if there had only been a little longer, if she had only waited a little — and I would have dissipated the darkness! — It was not as though she had not recovered her calmness. The very next day she listened to me with a smile, in spite of her confusion. . . . All this time, all these five days, she was either confused or ashamed. She was afraid, too, very much afraid. I don't dispute it, I am not so mad as to deny it. It was terror, but how could she help being frightened? We had so long been strangers to one another, had grown so alienated from one another, and suddenly all this. . . . But I did not look at her terror. I was dazzled by the new life beginning. . . ! It is true, it is undoubtedly true that I made a mistake. There were even, perhaps, many mistakes.

When I woke up next day, the first thing in the morning (that was on Wednesday), I made a mistake: I suddenly made her my friend. I was in too great a hurry, but a confession was necessary, inevitable — more than a confession! I did not even hide what I had hidden from myself all my life. I told her straight out that the whole winter I had been doing nothing but brood over the certainty of her love. I made clear to her that my money-lending had been simply the degradation of my will and my mind, my personal idea of self-castigation and self-exaltation. I explained to her that I really had been cowardly that time in the refreshment bar, that it was owing to my temperament, to my self-consciousness. I was impressed by the surroundings, by the theater: I was doubtful how I should succeed and whether it would be stupid. I was not afraid of a duel, but of its being stupid . . . and afterwards I would not own it and tormented everyone and had tormented her for it, and had married her so as to torment her for it. In fact, for the most part I talked as though in delirium. She herself took my hands and made me leave off. "You are exaggerating . . . you are distressing yourself," ad again there were tears, again almost hysterics! She kept begging me not to say all this, not to recall it.

I took no notice of her entreaties, or hardly noticed them: "Spring, Boulogne! There there would be sunshine, there our new sunshine," I kept saying that! I shut up the shop and transferred it to Dobronravov. I suddenly suggested to her giving all our money to the poor except the three thousand left me by my godmother, which we would spend on going to Boulogne, and then we would come back and begin a new life of real work. So we decided, for she said nothing. . . . She only smiled. And I believe she smiled chiefly from delicacy, for fear of disappointing me. I saw, of course, that I was burdensome to her, don't imagine I was so stupid or egoistic as not to see it. I saw it all, all, to the smallest detail, I saw better than anyone; all the hopelessness of my position stood revealed.

I told her everything about myself and about her. And about Lukerya. I told her that I had wept.... Oh, of course, I changed the conversation. I tried, too, not to say a word more about certain things. And, indeed, she did revive once or twice — I remember it, I remember it! Why do you say I looked at her and saw nothing? And if only this had not happened, everything would have come to life again. Why, only the day before yesterday, when we were talking of reading and what she had been reading that winter, she told me something herself, and laughed as she told me, recalling the scene of Gil Blas and the Archbishop of Granada. And with that sweet, childish laughter, just as in old days when we were eager (one instant! one instant!); how glad I was! I was awfully struck, though, by the story of the Archbishop; so she had found peace of mind and happiness enough to laugh at that literary masterpiece while she was sitting there in the winter. So then she had begun to be fully at rest, had begun to believe confidently "that I should leave her like that. I thought you would leave me like that," those were the word she uttered then on Tuesday! Oh! the thought of a child of ten! And you know she believed it, she believed that really everything would remain like that: she at her table and I at mine, and we both should go on like that till we were sixty. And all at once — I come forward, her husband, and the husband wants love! Oh, the delusion! Oh, my blindness!

It was a mistake, too, that I looked at her with rapture; I ought to have controlled myself, as it was my rapture frightened her. But, indeed, I did control myself, I did not kiss her feet again. I never made a sign of ... well, that I was her husband — oh, there was no thought of that in my mind, I only worshipped her! But, you know, I couldn't be quite silent, I could not refrain from speaking altogether! I suddenly said to her frankly, that I enjoyed her conversation and that I thought her incomparably more cultured and developed than I. She flushed crimson and said in confusion that I exaggerated. Then, like a fool, I could not resist telling her how delighted I had been when I had stood behind the door listening to her duel, the duel of innocence with that low cad, and how I had enjoyed her cleverness, the brilliance of her wit, and, at the same time, her childlike simplicity. She seemed to shudder all over, was murmuring again that I exaggerated, but suddenly her whole face darkened, she hit it in her hands and broke into sobs. . . . Then I could not restrain myself: again I fell at her feet, again I began kissing her feet, and again it ended in a fit of hysterics, just as on Tuesday. That was yesterday evening – and – in the morning. . . .

In the morning! Madman! why, that morning was today, just now, only just now!

Listen and try to understand: why, when we met by the samovar (it was after yesterday's hysterics), I was actually struck by her calmness, that is the actual fact! And all night I had been trembling with terror over what happened yesterday. But suddenly she came up to me and, clasping her hands (this morning, this morning!) began telling me that she was a criminal, that she knew it, that her crime had been torturing her all the winter, was torturing her now. . . . That she appreciated my generosity. . . . "I will be your faithful wife, I will respect you . . ."

Then I leapt up and embraced her like a madman. I kissed her, kissed her face, kissed her lips like a husband for the first time after a long separation. And why did I go out this morning, only two hours . . . our passports for abroad. . . . Oh, God! if only I had come back five minutes, only five minutes earlier. . . ! That crowd at our gates, those eyes all fixed upon me. Oh, God!

Lukerya says (oh! I will not let Lukerya go now for anything. She knows all about it, she has been here all the winter, she will tell me everything!), she says that when I had gone out of the house and only about twenty minutes before I came back — she suddenly went into our room to her mistress to ask her something, I don't remember what, and saw that her icon (that same icon of the Mother of God) had been taken down and was standing before her on the table, and her mistress seemed to have only just been praying before it. "What are you doing, mistress?" "Nothing, Lukerya, run along." "Wait a minute, Lukerya." "She came up and kissed me." "Are you happy, mistress?" I said. "Yes, Lukerya," and she smiled, but so strangely. So strangely that Lukerya went back ten minutes later to have a look at her.

"She was standing by the wall, close to the window, she had laid her arm against the wall, and her head was pressed on her arm, she was standing like that thinking. And she was standing so deep in thought that she did not hear me come and look at her from the other room. She seemed to be smiling — standing, thinking and smiling. I looked at her, turned softly and went out wondering to myself, and suddenly I heard the window opened. I went in at once to say: 'It's fresh, mistress; mind you don't catch cold,' and suddenly I saw she had got on the window and was standing there, her full height, in the open window, with her back to me, holding the icon in her hand. My heart sank on the spot. I cried, 'Mistress, mistress.' She heard, made a movement to turn back to me, but, instead of turning back, took a step forward, pressed the icon to her bosom, and flung herself out of window."

I only remember that when I went in at the gate she was still warm. The worst of it was they were all looking at me. At first they shouted and then suddenly they were silent, and then all of them moved away from me . . . and she was lying there with the icon. I remember, as it were, in a darkness, that I went up to her in silence and looked at her a long while. But all came round me and said something to me. Lukerya was there too, but I did not see her. She says she said something to me. I only remember that workman. He kept shouting to me that, "Only a handful of blood came from her mouth, a handful, a handful!" and he pointed to the blood on a stone. I believe I touched the blood with my finger, I smeared my finger, I looked at my finger (that I remember), and he kept repeating: "a handful, a handful!"

"What do you mean by a handful?" I yelled with all my might, I am told, and I lifted up my hands and rushed at him.

Oh, wild! wild! Delusion! Monstrous! Impossible!

Chapter IV

I Was Only Five Minutes Too Late

*I*s it not so? Is it likely? Can one really say it was possible? What for, why did this woman die?

Oh, believe me, I understand, but why she dies is still a question. She was frightened of my love, asked herself seriously whether to accept it or not, could not bear the question and preferred to die. I know, I know, no need to rack my brains: she had made too many promises, she was afraid she could not keep them — it is clear. There are circumstances about it quite awful.

For why did she die? That is still a question, after all. The question hammers, hammers at my brain. I would have left her like that if she had wanted to remain like that. She did not believe it, that's what it was! No — no. I am talking nonsense, it was not that at all. It was simply because with me she had to be honest — if she loved me, she would have had to love me altogether, and not as she would have loved the grocer. And as she was too chaste, too pure, to consent to such love as the grocer wanted she did not want to deceive me. Did not want to deceive me with half love, counterfeiting love, or a quarter love. They are honest, too honest, that is what it is! I wanted to instill breadth of heart in her, in those days, do you remember? A strange idea.

It is awfully interesting to know: did she respect me or not? I don't know whether she despised me or not. I don't believe she did despise me. It is awfully strange: why did it never once enter my head all the winter that she despised me? I was absolutely convinced of the contrary up to that moment when she looked at me with stern surprise. Stern it was. I understood once for all, forever! Ah, let her, let her despise me all her life even, only let her be living! Only yesterday she was walking about, talking. I simply can't understand how she threw herself out of window! And how could I have imagined it five minutes before? I have called Lukerya. I won't let Lukerya go now for anything!

Oh, we might still have understood each other! We had simply become terribly estranged from one another during the winter, but couldn't we have grown used to each other again? Why, why, couldn't we have come together again and begun a new life again? I am generous, she was too — that was a point in common! Only a few more words, another two days — no more, and she would have understood everything.

What is most mortifying of all is that it is chance — simply a barbarous, lagging chance. that is what is mortifying! Five minutes, only five minutes too late! Had I come five minutes earlier, the moment would have passed away like a cloud, and it would never have entered her head again. And it would have ended by her understanding it all. But now again empty rooms, and me alone. Here the pendulum is ticking; it does not care, it has no pity. . . . There is no one — that's the misery of it!

I keep walking about, I keep walking about. I know, I know, you need not tell me; it amuses you, you think it absurd that I complain of chance and those five minutes. But it is evident. Consider one thing: she did not even leave a note, to say, "Blame no one for my death," as people always do. Might she not have thought that Lukerya might get into trouble. "She was alone with her," might have been said, "and pushed her out." In any case she would have been taken up by the police if it had not happened that four people, from the windows, from the lodge, and from the yard, had seen her stand with the icon in her hands and jump out of herself. But that, too, was a chance, that the people were standing there and saw her. No, it was all a moment, only an irresponsible moment. A sudden impulse, a fantasy! What if she did pray before the icon? It does not follow that she was facing death. The whole impulse lasted, perhaps, only some ten minutes; it was all decided, perhaps, while she stood against the wall with her head on her arm, smiling. The idea darted into her brain, she turned giddy and — and could not resist it.

Say what you will, it was clearly misunderstanding. It could have been possible to live with me. And what if it were anemia? Was it simply from poorness of blood, from the flagging of vital energy? She had grown tired during the winter, that was what it was. . . .

I was too late!

How thin she is in her coffin, how sharp her nose has grown! Her eyelashes lie straight as arrows. And, you know, when she fell, nothing was crushed, nothing was broken! Nothing but that "handful of blood." A dessertspoonful, that is. From internal injury. A strange thought: if only it were possible not to bury her? For if they take her away, then . . . oh, no, it is almost incredible that they take her away! I am not mad and I am not raving — on the contrary, my mind was never so lucid — but what shall I do when again there is no one, only the two rooms, and me alone with the pledges? Madness, madness, madness! I worried her to death, that is what it is!

What are your laws to me now? What do I care for your customs, your morals, your life, your state, your faith! Let your judge judge me, let me be brought before your court, let me be tried by jury, and I shall say that I admit nothing. the judge will shout, "Be silent, officer." And I will shout to him, "What power have you now that I will obey? Why did blind, inert force destroy that which was dearest of all? What are your laws to me now? They are nothing to me." Oh, I don't care!

She was blind, blind! She is dead, she does not hear! You do not know with what paradise I would have surrounded you. There was paradise in my soul, I would have made it blossom around you! Well, you wouldn't have loved me — so be it, what of it? Things should still have been like that, everything should have remained like that. You should only have talked to me as a friend — we could have rejoiced and laughed with joy looking at one another. And so we should have lived. And if you had loved another — well, so be it, so be it! You should have walked with him laughing, and I should have watched you from the other side of the street. . . . Oh, anything, anything, if only she would open her eyes just once! For one instant, only one! If she would look at me as she did this morning, when she stood before me and made a vow to be a faithful wife! Oh, in one look she would have understood it all!

Oh, blind force! Oh, nature! Men are alone on earth — that is what is dreadful! "Is there a living man in the country?" cried the Russian hero. I cry the same, though I am not a hero, and no one answers my cry.

They say the sun gives life to the universe. The sun is rising and — look at it, is it not dead? Everything is dead and everywhere there are dead. Men are alone — around them is silence — that is the earth! "Men, love one another" — who said that? Whose commandment is that? The pendulum ticks callously, heartlessly. Two o'clock at night. Her little shoes are standing by the little bed, as though waiting for her. . . . No, seriously, when they take her away tomorrow, what will become of me?

The Little Orphan*

I

*I*N a large city, on Christmas eve in the biting cold, I see a young child, still quite young, six years old, perhaps even less; yet too young to be sent on the street begging, but assuredly destined to be sent in a year or two.

This child awakes one morning in a damp and frosty

---

* From *The Cosmopolitan,* published by Schlicht & Field, Co. of Rochester, N.Y. In February 1887. This story is an excellent example of the style of M. Dostoevsky, the great Russian novelist, whose works are attracting so much attention in France. It is without plot, like most of his stories, but it is a very powerful and realistic sketch. The repetition of words and phrases noticeable in this story is common to Russian stories. It is particularly noticeable in Count Leon Tolstoy's "Search for Happiness," a volume of short stories written for the Russian peasants.

cellar. He is wrapped in a kind of squalid dressing gown and is shivering. His breath issues from between his lips in white vapor; he is seated on a trunk; to pass the time he blows the breath from his mouth, and amuses himself in seeing it escape. But he is very hungry. Several times since morning he has drawn near the bed covered with a straw mattress as thin as gauze, where his mother lies sick, her head resting on a bundle of rags instead of a pillow.

How did she come there? She came probably from a strange city and has fallen ill. The proprietress of the miserable lodging was arrested two days ago, and carried to the police station; it is a holiday today, and the other tenants have gone out. However, one of them has remained in bed for the last twenty-four hours, stupid with drink, not having waited for the holiday.

From another corner issue the complaints of an old woman of eighty years, laid up with rheumatism. This old woman was formerly a children's nurse somewhere; now she is dying all alone. She whines, moans, and growls at the little boy, who begins to be afraid to come near the corner where she lies with the death rattle in her throat. He has found something to drink in the hallway, but he has not been able to lay his hand on the smallest crust of bread, and for the tenth time he comes to wake his mother. He finishes by getting frightened in this darkness.

The evening is already late, and no one comes to kindle the fire. He finds, by feeling around, his mother's face, and is astonished that she no longer moves and that she has become as cold as the wall.

"It is so cold!" he thinks.

He remains some time without moving, his hand resting on the shoulder of the corpse. Then he begins to blow in his fingers to warm them, and, happening to find his little cap on the bed, he looks softly for the door, and issues forth from the underground lodging.

He would have gone out sooner had he not been afraid of the big dog that barks all the day up there on the landing before their neighbor's door.

Oh! what a city! never before had he seen anything like it. Down yonder from where he came, the nights are much darker. There is only one lamp for the whole street; little low wooden houses, closed with shutters; in the street from the time it grows dark, no one; everyone shut up at home: only a crowd of dogs that howl, hundreds, thousands of dogs, that howl and bark all the night. But then, it used to be so warm there! And he got something to eat. Here, ah! how good it would be to have something to eat! What a noise here, what an uproar! What a great light, and what a crowd of people! What horses, and what carriages! And the cold, the cold! The bodies of the tired horses smoke with frost and their burning nostrils puff white clouds; their shoes ring on the pavement through the soft snow. And how everybody hustles everybody else! "Ah! how I would like to eat a little piece of something. That is what makes my fingers ache so."

II

A POLICEMAN just passes by, and turns his head so as not to see the child.

"Here is another street. Oh! how wide it is! I shall be crushed to death here, I know; how they all shout, how they run, how they roll along! And the light, and the light! And that, what is that? Oh! what a big window-pane! And behind the pane, a room, and in the room a tree that goes up to the ceiling; it is the Christmas tree. And what lights under the tree! Such papers of gold, and such apples! And all around dolls and little hobby-horses. There are little children well-dressed, nice, and clean; they are laughing and playing, eating and drinking things. There is a little girl going to dance with the little boy. How pretty she is! And there is music. I can hear it through the glass."

The child looks, admires, and even laughs. He feels no longer any pain in his fingers or feet. The fingers of his hand have become all red, he cannot bend them anymore, and it hurts him to move them. But all at once, he feels that his fingers ache; he begins to cry, and goes away. He perceives through another window another room, and again trees and cakes of all sorts on the table, red almonds and yellow ones. Four beautiful ladies are sitting down, and when any body comes he is given some cake: and the door opens every minute, and many gentlemen enter. The little fellow crept forward, opened the door of a sudden, and went in. Oh! what a noise was made when they saw him, what confusion! Immediately a lady arose, put a kopeck in his hand, and opened herself the street door for him. How frightened he was!

III

*T*HE kopeck has fallen from his hands, and rings

on the steps of the stairs. He was not able to tighten his little fingers enough to hold the coin. The child went out running, and walked fast, fast. Where was he going? He did not know. And he runs, runs, and blows in his hands. He is troubled. He feels so lonely, so frightened! And suddenly, what is that again! A crowd of people stand there and admire.

"A window! behind the pane, three pretty dolls attired in wee red and yellow dresses, and just exactly as though they were alive! And that little old man sitting down, who seems to play the fiddle. There are two others, too, standing up, who play on tiny violins, keeping time with their heads to the music. They look at each other and their lips move. And they really speak? Only they cannot be heard through the glass."

And the child first thinks that they are living, and when he comprehends that they are only dolls, he begins to laugh. Never had he seen such dolls before, and he didn't know that there were any like that! He would like to cry, but those dolls are just too funny!

IV

SUDDENLY he feels himself seized by the coat. A big rough boy stands near him, who gives him a blow of his fist on the head, snatches his cap, and trips him up.

The child falls. At the same time there is a shout; he remains a moment paralyzed with fear. Then he springs up with a bound and runs, runs, darts under a gateway somewhere and hides himself in a courtyard behind a pile of wood. He cowers and shivers in his fright; he can hardly breathe.

And suddenly he feels quite comfortable. His little hands and feet don't hurt anymore; he is warm, warm as though near a stove, and all his body trembles.

"Ah! I am going asleep! how nice it is to have a sleep! I shall stay a little while and then I will go and see the dolls again," thought the little fellow, and he smiled at the recollection of the dolls. "They looked just as though they were alive!"

Then he hears his mother's song. "Mamma, I am going to sleep. Ah! how nice it is here for sleeping!"

"Come to my house, little boy, to see the Christmas tree," said a soft voice.

He thought at first it was his mother; but no, it was not she.

Then who is calling him? He does not see. But some one stoops over him, and folds him in his arms in the darkness: and he stretches out his hand and — all at once — oh! what light! Oh! what a Christmas tree! No, it is not a Christmas tree; he has never seen the like of it!

Where is he now? All is resplendent, all is radiant, and dolls all around; but no, not dolls, little boys, little girls; only they are very bright. All of them circle round him; they fly. They hug him, they take him and carry him away, and he is flying too. And he sees his mother looking at him and laughing joyfully.

"Mamma! mamma! ah! how nice it is here!" cries her little boy to her.

And again he embraces the children, and would like very much to tell them about the dolls behind the windowpane. "Who are you, little girls?" he asks, laughing and fondling them.

It is the Christmas tree at Jesus's.

At Jesus's, that day, there is always a Christmas tree for little children that have none themselves.

And he learned that all these little boys and girls were children like himself, who had died like him. Some had died of cold in the baskets abandoned at the doors of the public functionaries of St. Petersburg; others had died out at nurse in the foul hovels of the Tchaukhnas; others of hunger at the dry breasts of their mothers during the famine. All were here now, all little angels now, all with Jesus, and He Himself among them, spreading his hands over them, blessing them and their sinful mothers.

And the mothers of these children are there too, apart, weeping; each recognizes her son or her daughter, and the children fly towards them, embrace them, wipe away the tears with their little hands, and beg them not to weep.

And below on the earth, the concierge in the morning found the wee corpse of the child, who had taken refuge in the courtyard. Stiff and frozen behind the pile of wood it lay.

The mother was found too. She died before him; both are reunited in Heaven in the Lord's house.

The Peasant Marey*

But reading all these professions de foi is a bore, I think, and so I'll tell you a story; actually, it's not even a story, but only a reminiscence of something that happened long ago and that, for some reason, I would very much like to recount here and now, as a conclusion to our treatise on the People. At the time I was only nine years old. . . . But no, I'd best begin with the time I was twenty-nine.

It was the second day of Easter Week. The air was warm, the sky was blue, the sun was high, warm, and bright, but there was only gloom in my heart. I was wandering behind the prison barracks, examining and counting off the pales in the sturdy prison stockade, but I had lost even the desire to count, although such was my habit. It was the second day of "marking the holiday" within the prison compound; the prisoners

---

* Translated by Kenneth Lantz, from *Diary of a Writer,* Feb. 1876

were not taken out to work; many were drunk; there were shouts of abuse, and quarrels were constantly breaking out in all corners. Disgraceful, hideous songs; card games in little nooks under the bunks; a few convicts, already beaten half to death by sentence of their comrades for their particular rowdiness, lay on bunks covered with sheepskin coats until such time as they might come to their senses; knives had already been drawn a few times — all this, in two days of holiday, had worn me out to the point of illness. Indeed, I never could endure the drunken carousals of peasants without being disgusted, and here, in this place, particularly. During these days even the prison staff did not look in; they made no searches, nor did they check for alcohol, for they realized that once a year they had to allow even these outcasts to have a spree; otherwise it might be even worse. At last, anger welled up in my heart. I ran across the Pole Macki, a political prisoner; he gave me a gloomy look, his eyes glittering and his lips trembling: "Je hais ces brigands!" he muttered, gritting his teeth, and passed me by. I returned to the barrack despite the fact that a quarter-hour before I had fled half-demented when six healthy peasants had thrown themselves as one man, on the drunken Tatar Gazin and had begun beating him to make him settle down; they beat him senselessly with such blows as might have killed a camel; but they knew that it was not easy to kill this Hercules and so they didn't hold back. And now when I returned to the barracks I noticed Gazin lying senseless on a bunk in the corner showing scarcely any signs of life; he was lying under a sheepskin coat, and everyone passed him by in silence: although they firmly hoped he would revive the next morning, still, "with a beating like that, God forbid, you could finish a man off." I made my way to my bunk opposite a window with an iron grating and lay down on my back, my hands behind my head, and closed my eyes. I liked to lie like that: a sleeping man was left alone, while at the same time one could daydream and think. But dreams did not come to me; my heart beat restlessly and Macki's words kept echoing in my ears: "je hais ces brigands!" However, why describe my feelings? Even now at night I sometimes dream of that time, and none of my dreams are more agonizing. Perhaps you will also notice that until today I have scarcely ever spoken in print of my prison life; I wrote Notes from the House of the Dead fifteen years ago using an invented narrator, a criminal who supposedly had murdered his wife. (I might add, by the way, that many people supposed and are even now quite firmly convinced that I was sent to hard labor for the murder of my wife.) Little by little I lost myself in reverie and imperceptibly sank into memories of the past. All through my four years in prison I continually thought of all my past days, and I think I relived the whole of my former life in my memories. These memories arose in my mind of themselves; rarely did I summon them up consciously. They would begin from a certain point, some little thing that was often barely perceptible, and then bit by bit they would grow into a finished picture, some strong and complete impression. I would analyze these impressions, adding new touches to things experienced long ago; and the main thing was that I would refix them, continually refine them, and in this consisted my entire entertainment. This time, for some reason, I suddenly recalled a moment of no apparent significance from my early childhood when I was only nine years old, a moment that I thought I had completely forgotten; but at that time I was particularly fond of memories of my very early childhood. I recalled one August at our home in the country: the day was clear and dry, but a bit chilly and windy; summer was on the wane, and soon I would have to go back to Moscow to spend the whole winter in boredom over my French lessons; and I was so sorry to have to leave the country. I passed by the granaries, made my way down into the gully, and climbed up into the Dell — that was what we called a thick patch of bushes that stretched from the far side of the gully to a grove of trees. And so I make my way deeper into the bushes and can hear that some thirty paces away a solitary peasant is plowing in the clearing. I know he's plowing up the steep side of a hill and his horse finds it heavy going; from time to time I hear his shout, "Gee-up!" I know almost all our peasants, but don't recognize the one who's plowing; and what difference does it make, anyway, since I'm quite absorbed in my own business. I also have an occupation: I'm breaking off a switch of walnut to lash frogs; walnut switches are so lovely and quite without flaws, so much better than birch ones I'm also busy with bugs and beetles, collecting them; some are very pretty; I love the small, nimble, red-and-yellow lizards with the little black spots as well, but I'm afraid of snakes. I come across snakes far less often than lizards, however. There aren't many mushrooms here; you have to go into the birch wood for mushrooms, and that's what I have in mind. I liked nothing better than the forest with its mushrooms and wild berries, its insects, and its birds, hedgehogs, and squirrels, and with its damp aroma of rotting leaves that I loved so. And even now, as I write this, I can catch the fragrance from our stand of birches in the country: these impressions stay with you all your life. Suddenly, amid the deep silence, I clearly and distinctly heard a shout: "There's a wolf!" I screamed, and, beside myself with terror, crying at the top of my voice, I ran out into the field, straight at the plowing peasant.

It was our peasant Marey. I don't know if there is such a name, but everyone called him Marey. He was a man of about fifty, heavyset, rather tall, with heavy streaks of grey in his bushy, dark-brown beard. I knew him but had scarcely ever had occasion to speak to him before. He even stopped his little filly when he heard my cry, and when I rushed up to him and seized his plow with one hand and his sleeve with the other, he saw how terrified I was.

"It's a wolf!" I cried, completely out of breath.

Instinctively he jerked his head to look around, for an instant almost believing me.

"Where's the wolf?"

"I heard a shout. . . . Someone just shouted, 'Wolf'" . . I babbled.

"What do you mean, lad? There's no wolf; you're just hearing," reassuring me. But I was all a-tremble and clung to his coat sleeve, more tightly; I suppose I was very pale as well. He looked at me with an uneasy smile, evidently concerned and alarmed for me.

"Why you took a real fright, you did!" he said, wagging his head. "Never mind, now, my dear. What a fine lad you are!"

He stretched out his hand and suddenly stroked my cheek.

"Never mind, now, there's nothing to be afraid of. Christ be with you. Cross yourself, lad." But I couldn't cross myself; the corners of my mouth were trembling, and I think this particularly struck him. He quietly stretched out a thick, earth-soiled finger with a black nail and gently touched it to my trembling lips.

"Now, now," he smiled at me with a broad, almost maternal smile. "Lord, what a dreadful fuss. Dear, dear, dear!"

At last I realized that there was no wolf and that I must have imagined hearing the cry of "Wolf." Still, it had been such a clear and distinct shout; two or three times before, however, I had imagined such cries (not only about wolves), and I was aware of that. (Later, when childhood passed, these hallucinations did as well.)

"Well, I'll be off now," I said, making it seem like a question and looking at him shyly.

"Off with you, then, and I'll keep an eye on you as you go. Can't let the wolf get you!" he added, still giving me a maternal smile. "Well, Christ be with you, off you go." He made the sign of the cross over me, and crossed himself I set off, looking over my shoulder almost every ten steps. Marey continued to stand with his little filly, looking after me and nodding every time I looked around. I confess I felt a little ashamed at taking such a fright. But I went on, still with a good deal of fear of the wolf, until I had gone up the slope of the gully to the first threshing barn; and here the fear vanished entirely, and suddenly our dog Volchok came dashing out to meet me. With Volchok I felt totally reassured and I turned toward Marey for the last time; I could no longer make out his face clearly, but I felt that he was still smiling kindly at me and nodding. I waved to him, and he returned my wave and urged on his little filly.

"Gee-up," came his distant shout once more, and his little filly once more started drawing the wooden plow.

*T*his memory came to me all at once — I don't know why — but with amazing clarity of detail. Suddenly I roused myself and sat on the bunk; I recall that a quiet smile of reminiscence still played on my face. I kept on recollecting for yet another minute. I remembered that when I had come home from Marey I told no one about my "adventure." And what kind of adventure was it anyway? I forgot about Marey very quickly as well. On the rare occasions when I met him later, I never struck up a conversation with him, either about the wolf or anything else, and now, suddenly, twenty years later, in Siberia, I remembered that encounter so vividly, right down to the last detail. That means it had settled unnoticed in my heart, all by itself with no will of mine, and had suddenly come back to me at a time when it was needed; I recalled the tender, maternal smile of a poor serf, the way he crossed me and shook his head: "Well you did take a fright now, didn't you, lad!" And I especially remember his thick finger, soiled with dirt, that he touched quietly and with shy tenderness to my trembling lips. Of course, anyone would try to reassure a child, but here in this solitary encounter something quite different had happened, and had I been his very own son he could not have looked at me with a glance that radiated more pure love, and who had prompted him to do that? He was our own serf, and I was his master's little boy; no one would learn of his kindness to me and reward him for it. Was he, maybe, especially fond of small children? There are such people. Our encounter was solitary, in an open field, and only God, perhaps, looking down saw what deep and enlightened human feeling and what delicate, almost feminine tenderness could fill the heart of a coarse, bestially ignorant Russian serf who at the time did not expect or even dream of his freedom. Now tell me, is this not what Konstantin Aksakov had in mind when he spoke of the advanced level of development of our Russian People?

And so when I climbed down from my bunk and looked around, I remember I suddenly felt I could regard these unfortunates in an entirely different way and that suddenly, through some sort of miracle, the former hatred and anger in my heart had vanished. I went off, peering intently into the faces of those I met. This disgraced peasant, with shaven head and brands on his cheek, drunk and roaring out his hoarse, drunken song — why he might also be that very same Marey; I cannot peer into his heart, after all. That same evening I met Macki once again. The unfortunate man! He had no recollections of any Mareys and no other view of these people but "Je hais ces brigands!" No, the Poles had to bear more than we did in those days!

The Dream of a Ridiculous Man[*]

I

I am a ridiculous person. Now they call me a madman. That would be a promotion if it were not that I remain as ridiculous in their eyes as before. But now I do not resent it, they are all dear to me now, even when they laugh at me — and, indeed, it is just then that they are particularly dear to me. I could join in their laughter — not exactly at myself, but through affection for them, if I did not feel so sad as I look at them. Sad

---

[*] Translated by Constance Garnett.

because they do not know the truth and I do know it. Oh, how hard it is to be the only one who knows the truth! But they won't understand that. No, they won't understand it.

In old days I used to be miserable at seeming ridiculous. Not seeming, but being. I have always been ridiculous, and I have known it, perhaps, from the hour I was born. Perhaps from the time I was seven years old I knew I was ridiculous. Afterwards I went to school, studied at the university, and, do you know, the more I learned, the more thoroughly I understood that I was ridiculous. So that it seemed in the end as though all the sciences I studied at the university existed only to prove and make evident to me as I went more deeply into them that I was ridiculous. It was the same with life as it was with science. With every year the same consciousness of the ridiculous figure I cut in every relation grew and strengthened. Everyone always laughed at me. But not one of them knew or guessed that if there were one man on earth who knew better than anybody else that I was absurd, it was myself, and what I resented most of all was that they did not know that. But that was my own fault; I was so proud that nothing would have ever induced me to tell it to anyone. This pride grew in me with the years; and if it had happened that I allowed myself to confess to anyone that I was ridiculous, I believe that I should have blown out my brains the same evening. Oh, how I suffered in my early youth from the fear that I might give way and confess it to my schoolfellows. But since I grew to manhood, I have for some unknown reason become calmer, though I realized my awful characteristic more fully every year. I say 'unknown', for to this day I cannot tell why it was. Perhaps it was owing to the terrible misery that was growing in my soul through something which was of more consequence than anything else about me: that something was the conviction that had come upon me that nothing in the world mattered. I had long had an inkling of it, but the full realization came last year almost suddenly. I suddenly felt that it was all the same to me whether the world existed or whether there had never been anything at all: I began to feel with all my being that there was nothing existing. At first I fancied that many things had existed in the past, but afterwards I guessed that there never had been anything in the past either, but that it had only seemed so for some reason. Little by little I guessed that there would be nothing in the future either. Then I left off being angry with people and almost ceased to notice them. Indeed this showed itself even in the pettiest trifles: I used, for instance, to knock against people in the street. And not so much from being lost in thought: what had I to think about? I had almost given up thinking by that time; nothing mattered to me. If at least I had solved my problems! Oh, I had not settled one of them, and how many there were! But I gave up caring about anything, and all the problems disappeared.

And it was after that that I found out the truth. I learnt the truth last November — on the third of November, to be precise — and I remember every instant since. It was a gloomy evening, one of the gloomiest possible evenings. I was going home at about eleven o'clock, and I remember that I thought that the evening could not be gloomier. Even physically. Rain had been falling all day, and it had been a cold, gloomy, almost menacing rain, with, I remember, an unmistakable spite against mankind. Suddenly between ten and eleven it had stopped, and was followed by a horrible dampness, colder and damper than the rain, and a sort of steam was rising from everything, from every stone in the street, and from every by-lane if one looked down it as far as one could. A thought suddenly occurred to me, that if all the street lamps had been put out it would have been less cheerless, that the gas made one's heart sadder because it lighted it all up. I had had scarcely any dinner that day, and had been spending the evening with an engineer, and two other friends had been there also. I sat silent — I fancy I bored them. They talked of something rousing and suddenly they got excited over it. But they did not really care, I could see that, and only made a show of being excited. I suddenly said as much to them. "My friends," I said, "you really do not care one way or the other." They were not offended, but they laughed at me. That was because I spoke without any not of reproach, simply because it did not matter to me. They saw it did not, and it amused them.

As I was thinking about the gas lamps in the street I looked up at the sky. The sky was horribly dark, but one could distinctly see tattered clouds, and between them fathomless black patches. Suddenly I noticed in one of these patches a star, and began watching it intently. That was because that star had given me an idea: I decided to kill myself that night. I had firmly determined to do so two months before, and poor as I was, I bought a splendid revolver that very day, and loaded it. But two months had passed and it was still lying in my drawer; I was so utterly indifferent that I wanted to seize a moment when I would not be so indifferent — why, I don't know. And so for two months every night that I came home I thought I would shoot myself. I kept waiting for the right moment. And so now this star gave me a thought. I made up my mind that it should certainly be that night. And why the star gave me the thought I don't know.

And just as I was looking at the sky, this little girl took me by the elbow. The street was empty, and there was scarcely anyone to be seen. A cabman was sleeping in the distance in his cab. It was a child of eight with a kerchief on her head, wearing nothing but a wretched little dress all soaked with rain, but I noticed her wet broken shoes and I recall them now. They caught my eye particularly. She suddenly pulled me by the elbow and called me. She was not weeping, but was spasmodically crying out some words which could not utter properly, because she was shivering and shuddering all over. She was in terror about something, and kept crying, "Mammy, mammy!" I turned facing her, I did not say a word and went on; but she ran, pulling at me, and there was that note in her voice which in frightened children means despair. I know that sound. Though she did not articulate the words, I understood that her mother was dying, or that something of the sort was happening to them, and that she had run out to call someone, to find something to help her mother. I did not go with her; on the contrary, I had an impulse to drive her away. I told her first to go to a policeman. But clasping her hands, she ran beside me sobbing and gasping, and would not leave me. Then I stamped my foot and shouted at her. She called out "Sir! sir. . . !" but suddenly abandoned me and rushed headlong across the road. Some other passerby appeared there, and she evidently flew from me to him.

I mounted up to my fifth storey. I have a room in a flat where there are other lodgers. My room is small and poor, with a garret window in the shape of a semicircle. I have a sofa covered with American leather, a table with books on it, two chairs and a comfortable armchair, as old as old can be, but of the good old-fashioned shape. I sat down, lighted the candle, and began thinking. In the room next to mine, through the partition wall, a perfect Bedlam was going on. It had been going on for the last three days. A retired captain lived there, and he had half a dozen visitors, gentlemen of doubtful reputation, drinking vodka and playing stoss with old cards. The night before there had been a fight, and I know that two of them had been for a long time engaged in dragging each other about by the hair. The landlady wanted to complain, but she was in abject terror of the captain. There was only one other lodger in the flat, a thin little regimental lady, on a visit to Petersburg, with three little children who had been taken ill since they came into the lodgings. Both she and her children were in mortal fear of the captain, and lay trembling and crossing themselves all night, and the youngest child had a sort of fit from fright. That captain, I know for a fact, sometimes stops people in the Nevsky Prospect and begs. They won't take him into the service, but strange to say (that's why I am telling this), all this month that the captain has been here his behavior has caused me no annoyance. I have, of course, tried to avoid his acquaintance from the very beginning, and he, too, was bored with me from the first; but I never care how much they shout the other side of the partition nor how many of them there are in there: I sit up all night and forget them so completely that I do not even hear them. I stay awake till daybreak, and have been going on like that for the last year. I sit up all night in my armchair at the table, doing nothing. I only read by day. I sit — don't even think; ideas of a sort wander through my mind and I let them come and go as they will. A whole candle is burned every night. I sat down quietly at the table, took out the revolver and put it down before me. When I had put it down I asked myself, I remember, "Is that so?" and answered with complete conviction, "It is." That is, I shall shoot myself. I knew that I should shoot myself that night for certain, but how much longer I should go on sitting at the table I did not know. And no doubt

I should have shot myself if it had not been for that little girl.

II

You see, though nothing mattered to me, I could feel pain, for instance. If anyone had stuck me it would have hurt me. It was the same morally: if anything very pathetic happened, I should have felt pity just as I used to do in old days when there were things in life that did matter to me. I had felt pity that evening. I should have certainly helped a child. Why, then, had I not helped the little girl? Because of an idea that occurred to me at the time: when she was calling and pulling at me, a question suddenly arose before me and I could not settle it. The question was an idle one, but I was vexed. I was vexed at the reflection that if I were going to make an end of myself that night, nothing in life ought to have mattered to me. Why was it that all at once I did not feel a strange pang, quite incongruous in my position. Really I do not know better how to convey my fleeting sensation at the moment, but the sensation persisted at home when I was sitting at the table, and I was very much irritated as I had not been for a long time past. One reflection followed another. I saw clearly that so long as I was still a human being and not nothingness, I was alive and so could suffer, be angry and feel shame at my actions. So be it. But if I am going to kill myself, in two hours, say, what is the little girl to me and what have I to do with shame or with anything else in the world? I shall turn into nothing, absolutely nothing. And can it really be true that the consciousness that I shall completely cease to exist immediately and so everything else will cease to exist, does not in the least affect my feeling of pity for the child nor the feeling of shame after a contemptible action? I stamped and shouted at the unhappy child as though to say — not only I feel no pity, but even if I behave inhumanly and contemptibly, I am free to, for in another two hours everything will be extinguished. Do you believe that that was why I shouted that? I am almost convinced of it now. I seemed clear to me that life and the world somehow depended upon me now. I may almost say that the world now seemed created for me alone: if I shot myself the world would cease to be at least for me. I say nothing of its being likely that nothing will exist for anyone when I am gone, and that as soon as my consciousness is extinguished the whole world will vanish too and become void like a phantom, as a mere appurtenance of my consciousness, for possibly all this world and all these people are only me myself. I remember that as I sat and reflected, I turned all these new questions that swarmed one after another quite the other way, and thought of something quite new. For instance, a strange reflection suddenly occurred to me, that if I had lived before on the moon or on Mars and there had committed the most disgraceful and dishonorable action and had there been put to such shame and ignominy as one can only conceive and realize in dreams, in nightmares, and if, finding myself afterwards on earth, I were able to retain the memory of what I had done on the other planet and at the same time knew that I should never, under any circumstances, return there, then looking from the earth to the moon — should I care or not? Should I feel shame for that action or not? These were idle and superfluous questions for the revolver was already lying before me, and I knew in every fiber of my being that it would happen for certain, but they excited me and I raged. I could not die now without having first settled something. In short, the child had saved me, for I put off my pistol shot for the sake of these questions. Meanwhile the clamor had begun to subside in the captain's room: they had finished their game, were settling down to sleep, and meanwhile were grumbling and languidly winding up their quarrels. At that point, I suddenly fell asleep in my chair at the table — a thing which had never happened to me before. I dropped asleep quite unawares.

Dreams, as we all know, are very queer things: some parts are presented with appalling vividness, with details worked up with the elaborate finish of jewelry, while others one gallops through, as it were, without noticing them at all, as, for instance, through space and time. Dreams seem to be spurred on not by reason but by desire, not by the head but by the heart, and yet what complicated tricks my reason has played sometimes in dreams, what utterly incomprehensible things happen to it! My brother died five years ago, for instance. I sometimes dream of him; he takes part in my affairs, we are very much interested, and yet all through my dream I quite know and remember that my brother is dead and buried. How is it that I am not surprised that, though he is dead, he is here beside me and working with me? Why is it that my reason fully accepts it? But enough. I will begin about my dream. Yes, I dreamed a dream, my dream of the third of November. They tease me now, telling me it was only a dream. But does it matter whether it was a dream or reality, if the dream made known to me the truth? If once one has recognized the truth and seen it, you know that it is the truth and that there is no other and there cannot be, whether you are asleep or awake. Let it be a dream, so be it, but that real life of which you make so much I had meant to extinguish by suicide, and my dream, my dream — oh, it revealed to me a different life, renewed, grand and full of power!

Listen.

III

I have mentioned that I dropped asleep unawares and even seemed to be still reflecting on the same subjects. I suddenly dreamt that I picked up the revolver and aimed it straight at my heart — my heart, and not my head; and I had determined beforehand to fire at my head, at my right temple. After aiming at my chest I waited a second or two, and suddenly my candle, my table, and the wall in front of me began moving and heaving. I made haste to pull the trigger.

In dreams you sometimes fall from a height, or are stabbed, or beaten, but you never feel pain unless, perhaps, you really bruise yourself against the bedstead, then you feel pain and almost always wake up from it. It was the same in my dream. I did not feel any pain, but it seemed as though with my shot everything within me was shaken and everything was suddenly dimmed, and it grew horribly black around me. I seemed to be blinded, and it benumbed, and I was lying on something hard, stretched on my back; I saw nothing, and could not make the slightest movement. People were walking and shouting around me, the captain bawled, the landlady shrieked — and suddenly another break and I was being carried in a closed coffin. And I felt how the coffin was shaking and reflected upon it, and for the first time the idea struck me that I was dead, utterly dead, I knew it and had no doubt of it, I could neither see nor move and yet I was feeling and reflecting. But I was soon reconciled to the position, and as one usually does in a dream, accepted the facts without disputing them.

And now I was buried in the earth. They all went away, I was left alone, utterly alone. I did not move. Whenever before I had imagined being buried the one sensation I associated with the grave was that of damp and cold. So now I felt that I was very cold, especially the tips of my toes, but I felt nothing else.

I lay still, strange to say I expected nothing, accepting without dispute that a dead man had nothing to expect. But it was damp. I don't know how long a time passed — whether an hour or several days, or many days. But all at once a drop of water fell on my closed left eye, making its way through the coffin lid; it was followed a minute later by a second, then a minute later by a third — and so on, regularly every minute. There was a sudden glow of profound indignation in my heart, and I suddenly felt in it a pang of physical pain. "That's my wound," I thought; "that's the bullet . . ." And drop after drop every minute kept falling on my closed eyelid. And all at once, not with my voice, but with my entire being, I called upon the power that was responsible for all that was happening to me:

"Whoever you may be, if you exist, and if anything more rational that what is happening here is possible, suffer it to be here now. But if you are revenging yourself upon me for my senseless suicide by the hideousness and absurdity of this subsequent existence, then let me tell you that no torture could ever equal the contempt which I shall go on dumbly feeling, though my martyrdom may last a million years!"

I made this appeal and held my peace. There was a full minute of unbroken silence and again another drop fell, but I knew with infinite unshakable certainty that everything would change immediately. And behold my grave suddenly was rent asunder, that is, I don't know whether it was opened or dug up, but I was caught up by some dark and unknown being and we found ourselves in space. I suddenly regained my sight. It was the dead of night, and never, never had there been such darkness. We were flying through space far away from the earth. I did not question the being who was taking me; I was proud and waited. I assured myself that I was not afraid, and was thrilled with ecstasy at the thought that I was not afraid. I do not know how long we were flying, I cannot imagine; it happened as it always does in dreams when you skip over space and time, and the laws of thought and existence, and only pause upon the points for which the heart yearns. I remember that I suddenly saw in the darkness a star. "Is that Sirius?" I asked impulsively, though I had not meant to ask questions.

"No, that is the star you saw between the clouds when you were coming home," the being who was carrying me replied.

I knew that it had something like a human face. Strange to say, I did not like that being, in fact I felt an intense aversion for it. I had expected complete non-existence, and that was why I had put a bullet through my heart. And here I was in the hands of a creature not human, of course, but yet living, existing. "And so there is life beyond the grave," I thought with the strange frivolity one has in dreams. But in its inmost depth my heart remained unchanged. "And if I have got to exist again," I thought, "and live once more under the control of some irresistible power, I won't be vanquished and humiliated."

"You know that I am afraid of you and despise me for that," I said suddenly to my companion, unable to refrain from the humiliating question which implied a confession, and feeling my humiliation stab my heart as with a pin. He did not answer my question, but all at once I felt that he was not even despising me, but was laughing at me and had no compassion for me, and that our journey had an unknown and mysterious object that concerned me only. Fear was growing in my heart. Something was mutely and painfully communicated to me from my silent companion, and permeated my whole being. We were flying through dark, unknown space. I had for some time lost sight of the constellations familiar to my eyes. I knew that there were stars in the heavenly spaces the light of which took thousands or millions of years to reach the earth. Perhaps we were already flying through those spaces. I expected something with a terrible anguish that tortured my heart. And suddenly I was thrilled by a familiar feeling that stirred me to the depths: I suddenly caught sight of our sun! I knew that it could not be our sun, that gave life to our earth, and that we were an infinite distance from our sun, but for some reason I knew in my whole being that it was a sun exactly like ours, a duplicate of it. A sweet, thrilling feeling resounded with ecstasy in my heart: the kindred power of the same light which had given me light stirred an echo in my heart and awakened it, and I had a sensation of life, the old life of the past for the first time since I had been in the grave.

"But if that is the sun, if that is exactly the same as our sun," I cried, "where is the earth?"

And my companion pointed to a star twinkling in the distance with an emerald light. We were flying straight towards it.

"And are such repetitions possible in the universe? Can that be the law of Nature. . . ? And if that is an earth there, can it be just the same earth as ours . . . just the same, as poor, as unhappy, but precious and beloved forever, arousing in the most ungrateful of her children the same poignant love for her that we feel for our earth?" I cried out, shaken by irresistible, ecstatic love for the old familiar earth which I had left. The image of the poor child whom I had repulsed flashed through my mind.

"You shall see it all," answered my companion, and there was a note of sorrow in his voice.

But we were rapidly approaching the planet. It was growing before my eyes; I could already distinguish the ocean, the outline of Europe; and suddenly a feeling of a great and holy jealousy glowed in my heart.

"How can it be repeated and what for? I love and can love only that earth which I have left, stained with my blood, when, in my ingratitude, I quenched my life with a bullet in my heart. But I have never, never ceased to love that earth, and perhaps on the very night I parted from it I loved it more than ever. Is there suffering upon this new earth? On our earth we can only love with suffering and through suffering. We cannot love otherwise, and we know of no other sort of love. I want suffering in order to love. I long, I thirst, this very instant, to kiss with tears the earth that I have left, and I don't want, I won't accept life on any other!"

But my companion had already left me. I suddenly, quite without noticing how, found myself on this other earth, in the bright light of a sunny day, fair as paradise. I believe I was standing on one of the islands that make up on our globe the Greek archipelago, or on the coast of the mainland facing that archipelago. Oh, everything was exactly as it is with us, only everything seemed to have a festive radiance, the splendor of some great, holy triumph attained at last. The caressing sea, green as emerald, splashed softly upon the shore and kissed it with manifest, almost conscious love. The tall, lovely trees stood in all the glory of their blossom, and their innumerable leaves greeted me, I am certain, with their soft, caressing rustle and seemed to articulate words of love. The grass glowed with bright and fragrant flowers. Birds were flying in flocks in the air, and perched fearlessly on my shoulders and arms and joyfully struck me with their darling, fluttering wings. And at last I saw and knew the people of this happy land. That came to me of themselves, they surrounded me, kissed me. The children of the sun, the children of their sun — oh, how beautiful they were! Never had I seen on our own earth such beauty in mankind. Only perhaps in our children, in their earliest years, one might find, some remote faint reflection of this beauty. The eyes of these happy people shone with a clear brightness. Their faces were radiant with the light of reason and fullness of a serenity that comes of perfect understanding, but those faces were gay; in their words and voices there was a note of childlike joy. Oh, from the first moment, from the first glance at them, I understood it all! It was the earth untarnished by the Fall; on it lived people who had not sinned. They lived just in such a paradise as that in which, according to all the legends of mankind, our first parents lived before they sinned; the only difference was that all this earth was the same paradise. These people, laughing joyfully, thronged round me and caressed me; they took me home with them, and each of them tried to reassure me. Oh, they asked me no questions, but they seemed, I fancied, to know everything without asking, and they wanted to make haste to smooth away the signs of suffering from my face.

IV

And do you know what? Well, granted that it was only a dream, yet the sensation of the love of those innocent and beautiful people has remained with me forever, and I feel as though their love is still flowing out to me from over there. I have seen them myself, have known them and been convinced; I loved them, I suffered for them afterwards. Oh, I understood at once even at the time that in many things I could not understand them at all; as an up-to-date Russian progressive and contemptible Petersburger, it struck me as inexplicable that, knowing so much, they had, for instance, no science like our. But I soon realized that their knowledge was gained and fostered by intuitions different from those of us on earth, and that their aspirations, too, were quite different. They desired nothing and were at peace; they did not aspire to knowledge of life as we aspire to understand it, because their lives were full. But their knowledge was higher and deeper than ours; for our science seeks to explain what life is, aspires to understand it in order to teach others how to love, while they without science knew how to live; and that I understood, but I could not understand their knowledge. They showed me their trees, and I could not understand the intense love with which they looked at them; it was as though they were talking with creatures like themselves. And perhaps I shall not be mistaken if I say that they conversed with them. Yes, they had found their language, and I am convinced that the trees understood them. They looked at all Nature like that — at the animals who lived in peace with them and did not attack them, but loved them, conquered by their love. They pointed to the stars and told me something about them which I could not understand, but I am convinced that they were somehow in touch with the stars, not only in thought, but by some living channel. Oh, these people did not persist in trying to make me understand them, they loved me without that, but I knew that they would never understand me, and so I hardly spoke to them about our earth. I only kissed in their presence the earth on which they lived and mutely worshipped them themselves. And they saw that and let me worship them without being abashed at my adoration, for they themselves loved much. They were not unhappy on my account when at times I kissed their feet with tears, joyfully conscious of the love with which they would respond to mine. At times I asked myself with wonder how it was they were able never to offend a creature like me, and never once to arouse a feeling of jealousy or envy in me? Often I wondered how it could be that, boastful and untruthful as I was, I never talked to them of what I knew — of which, of course, they had no notion — that I was never tempted to do so by a desire to astonish or even to benefit them.

They were as gay and sportive as children. They wandered about their lovely woods and copses, they sang their lovely songs; their fair was light — the fruits of their trees, the honey from their woods, and the milk of the animals who loved them. The work they did for food and raiment was brief and not laborious. They loved and begot children, but I never noticed in them the impulse of that cruel sensuality which overcomes almost every man on this earth, all and each, and is the source of almost every sin of mankind on earth. They rejoiced at the arrival of children as new beings to share their happiness. There was no quarreling, no jealousy among them, and they did not even know what the words meant. Their children were the children of all, for they all made up one family. There was scarcely any illness among them, though there was death; but their old people died peacefully, as though falling asleep, giving blessings and smiles to those who surrounded them to take their last farewell with bright and lovely smiles. I never saw grief or tears on those occasions, but only love, which reached the point of ecstasy, but a calm ecstasy, made perfect and contemplative. One might think that they were still in contact with the departed after death, and that their earthly union was not cut short by death. They scarcely understood me when I questioned them about immortality, but evidently they were so convinced of it without reasoning that it was not for them a question at all. They had no temples, but they had a real living and uninterrupted sense of oneness with the whole of the universe; they had no creed, but they had a certain knowledge that when their earthly joy had reached the limits of earthly nature, then there would come for them, for the living and for the dead, a still greater fullness of contact with the whole of the universe. They looked forward to that moment with joy, but without haste, not pining for it, but seeming to have a foretaste of it in their hearts, of which they talked to one another.

In the evening before going to sleep they liked singing in musical and harmonious chorus. In those songs they expressed all the sensations that the parting day had given them, sang its glories and took leave of it. They sang the praises of nature, of the sea, of the woods. They liked making songs about one another, and praised each other like children; they were the simplest songs, but they sprang from their hearts and went to one's heart. And not only in their songs but in all their lives they seemed to do nothing but admire one another. It was like being in love with each other, but an all-embracing, universal feeling.

Some of their songs, solemn and rapturous, I scarcely understood at all. Though I understood the words I could never fathom their full significance. It remained, as it were, beyond the grasp of my mind, yet my heart unconsciously absorbed it more and more. I often told them that I had had a presentiment of it long before, that this joy and glory had come to me on our earth in the form of a yearning melancholy that at times approached insufferable sorrow; that I had had a foreknowledge of them all and of their glory in the dreams of my heart and the visions of my mind; that often on our earth I could not look at the setting sun without tears . . . that in my hatred for the men of our earth there was always a yearning anguish: why could I not hate them without loving them? why could I not help forgiving them? and in my love for them there was a yearning grief: why could I not love them without hating them? They listened to me, and I saw they could not conceive what I was saying, but I did not regret that I had spoken to them of it: I knew that they understood the intensity of my yearning anguish over those whom I had left. But when they looked at me with their sweet eyes full of love, when I felt that in their presence my heart, too, became as innocent and just as theirs, the feeling of the fullness of life took my breath away, and I worshipped them in silence.

Oh, everyone laughs in my face now, and assures me that one cannot dream of such details as I am telling now, that I only dreamed or felt one sensation that arose in my heart in delirium and made up the details myself when I woke up. And when I told them that perhaps it really was so, my God, how they shouted with laughter in my face, and what mirth I caused! Oh, yes, of course I was overcome by the mere sensation of my dream, and that was all that was preserved in my cruelly wounded heart; but the actual forms and images of my dream, that is, the very ones I really saw at the very time of my dream, were filled with such harmony, were so lovely and enchanting and were so actual, that on awakening I was, of course, incapable of clothing them in our poor language, so that they were bound to become blurred in my mind; and so perhaps I really was forced afterwards to make up the details, and so of course to distort them in my passionate desire to convey some at least of them as quickly as I could. But on the other hand, how can I help believing that it was all true? It was perhaps a thousand times brighter, happier and more joyful than I describe it. Granted that I dreamed it, yet it must have been real. You know, I will tell you a secret: perhaps it was not a dream at all! For then something happened so awful, something so horribly true, that it could not have been imagined in a dream. My heart may have originated the dream, but would my heart alone have been capable of originating the awful event which happened to me afterwards? How could I alone have invented it or imagined it in my dream? Could my petty heart and fickle, trivial mind have risen to such a revelation of truth? Oh, judge for yourselves: hitherto I have concealed it, but now I will tell the truth. The fact is that I . . . corrupted them all!

V

Yes, yes, it ended in my corrupting them all! How it could come to pass I do not know, but I remember it clearly. The dream embraced thousands of years and left in me only a sense of the whole. I only know that I was the cause of their sin and downfall. Like a vile trichina, like a germ of the plague infecting whole kingdoms, so I contaminated all this earth, so happy and sinless before my coming. They learnt to lie, grew fond of lying, and discovered the charm of falsehood. Oh, at first perhaps it began innocently, with a jest, coquetry, with amorous play, perhaps indeed with a germ, but that germ of falsity made its way into their hearts and pleased them. Then sensuality was soon begotten, sensuality begot jealousy, jealousy — cruelty ... Oh, I don't know, I don't remember; but soon, very soon the first blood was shed. They marveled and were horrified, and began to be split up and divided. They formed into unions, but it was against one another. Reproaches, upbraidings followed. They came to know shame, and shame brought them to virtue. The conception of honor sprang up, and every union began waving its flags. They began torturing animals, and the animals withdrew from them into the forests and became hostile to them. They began to struggle for separation, for isolation, for individuality, for mine and thine. They began to talk in different languages. They became acquainted with sorrow and loved sorrow; they thirsted for suffering, and said that truth could only be attained through suffering. Then science appeared. As they became wicked they began talking of brotherhood and humanitarianism, and understood those ideas. As they became criminal, they invented justice and drew up whole legal codes in order to observe it, and to ensure their being kept, set up a guillotine. They hardly remembered what they had lost, in fact refused to believe that they had ever been happy and innocent. They even laughed at the possibility of this happiness in the past, and called it a dream. They could not even imagine it in definite form and shape, but, strange and wonderful to relate, though they lost all faith in their past happiness and called it a legend, they so longed to be happy and innocent once more that they succumbed to this desire like children, made an idol of it, set up temples and worshipped their own idea, their own desire; though at the same time they fully believed that it was unattainable and could not be realized, yet they bowed down to it and adored it with tears! Nevertheless, if it could have happened that they had returned to the innocent and happy condition which they had lost, and if someone had shown it to them again and had asked them whether they wanted to go back to it, they would certainly have refused. They answered me:

"We may be deceitful, wicked and unjust, we know it and weep over it, we grieve over it; we torment and punish ourselves more perhaps than that merciful Judge Who will judge us and whose Name we know not. But we have science, and by the means of it we shall find the truth and we shall arrive at it consciously. Knowledge is higher than feeling, the consciousness of life is higher than life. Science will give us wisdom, wisdom will reveal the laws, and the knowledge of the laws of happiness is higher than happiness."

That is what they said, and after saying such things everyone began to love himself better than anyone else, and indeed they could not do otherwise. All became so jealous of the rights of their own personality that they did their very utmost to curtail and destroy them in others, and made that the chief thing in their lives. Slavery followed, even voluntary slavery; the weak eagerly submitted to the strong, on condition that the latter aided them to subdue the still weaker. Then there were saints who came to these people, weeping, and talked to them of their pride, of their loss of harmony and due proportion, of their loss of shame. They were laughed at or pelted with stones. Holy blood was shed on the threshold of the temples. Then there arose men who began to think how to bring all people together again, so that everybody, while still loving himself best of all, might not interfere with others, and all might live together in something like a harmonious society. Regular wars sprang up over this idea. All the combatants at the same time firmly believed that science, wisdom and the instinct of self-preservation would force men at last to unite into a harmonious and rational society; and so, meanwhile, to hasten matters, 'the wise' endeavored to exterminate as rapidly as possible all who were 'not wise' and did not understand their idea, that the latter might not hinder its triumph. But the instinct of self-preservation grew rapidly weaker; there arose men, haughty and sensual, who demanded all or nothing. In order to obtain everything they resorted to crime, and if they did not succeed — to suicide. There arose religions with a cult of non-existence and self-destruction for the sake of the everlasting peace of annihilation. At last these people grew weary of their meaningless toil, and signs of suffering came into their faces, and then they proclaimed that suffering was a beauty, for in suffering alone was there meaning. They glorified suffering in their songs. I moved about among them, wringing my hands and weeping over them, but I loved them perhaps more than in old days when there was no suffering in their faces and when they were innocent and so lovely. I loved the earth they had polluted even more than when it had been a paradise, if only because sorrow had come to it. Alas! I always loved sorrow and tribulation, but only for myself, for myself; but I wept over them, pitying them. I stretched out my hands to them in despair, blaming, cursing and despising myself. I told them that all this was my doing, mine alone; that it was I had brought them corruption, contamination and falsity. I besought them to crucify me, I taught them how to make a cross. I could not kill myself, I had not the strength, but I wanted to suffer at their hands. I yearned for suffering, I longed that my blood should be drained to the last drop in these agonies. But they only laughed at me, and began at last to look upon me as crazy. They justified me, they declared that they had only got what they wanted themselves, and that all that now was could not have been otherwise. At last they declared to me that I was becoming dangerous and that they should lock me up in a madhouse if I did not hold my tongue. Then such grief took possession of my soul that my heart was wrung, and I felt as though I were dying; and then ... then I awoke.

It was morning, that is, it was not yet daylight, but about six o'clock. I woke up in the same armchair; my candle had burned out; everyone was asleep in the captain's room, and there was a stillness all round, rare in our flat. First of all I leapt up in great amazement: nothing like this had ever happened to me before, not even in the most trivial detail; I had never, for instance, fallen asleep like this in my armchair. While I was standing and coming to myself I suddenly caught sight of my revolver lying loaded, ready — but instantly I thrust it away! Oh, now, life, life! I lifted up my hands and called upon eternal truth, not with words, but with tears; ecstasy, immeasurable ecstasy flooded my soul.

Yes, life and spreading the good tidings! Oh, I at that moment resolved to spread the tidings, and resolved it, of course, for my whole life. I go to spread the tidings, I want to spread the tidings — of what? Of the truth, for I have seen it, have seen it with my own eyes, have seen it in all its glory.

And since then I have been preaching! Moreover I love all those who laugh at me more than any of the rest. Why that is so I do not know and cannot explain, but so be it. I am told that I am vague and confused, and if I am vague and confused now, what shall I be later on? It is true indeed: I am vague and confused, and perhaps as time goes on I shall be more so. And of course I shall make many blunders before I find out how to preach, that is, find out what words to say, what things to do, for it is a very difficult task. I see all that as clear as daylight, but, listen, who does not make mistakes? An yet, you know, all are making for the same goal, all are striving in the same direction anyway, from the sage to the lowest robber, only by different roads. It is an old truth, but this is what is new: I cannot go far wrong. For I have seen the truth; I have seen and I know that people can be beautiful and happy without losing the power of living on earth. I will not and cannot believe that evil is the normal condition of mankind. And it is just this faith of mine that they laugh at. But how can I help believing it? I have seen the truth — it is not as though I had invented it with my mind, I have seen it, seen it, and the living image of it has filled my soul forever. I have seen it in such full perfection that I cannot believe that it is impossible for people to have it. And so how can I go wrong? I shall make some slips no doubt, and shall perhaps talk in second-hand language, but not for long: the living image of what I saw will always be with me and will always correct and guide me. Oh, I am full of courage and freshness, and I will go on and on if it were for a thousand years! Do you know, at first I meant to conceal the fact that I corrupted them, but that was a mistake — that was my first mistake! But truth whispered to me that I was lying, and preserved me and corrected me. But how establish paradise — I don't know, because I do not know how to put it into words. After my dream I lost command of words. All the chief words, anyway, the most necessary ones. But never mind, I shall go and I shall keep talking, I won't leave off, for anyway I have seen it with my own eyes, though I cannot describe what I saw. But the scoffers do not understand that. It was a dream, they say, delirium, hallucination. Oh! As though that meant so much! And they are so proud! A dream! What is a dream? And is not our life a dream? I will say more. Suppose that this paradise will never come to pass (that I understand), yet I shall go on preaching it. And yet how simple it is: in one day, in one hour everything could be arranged at once! The chief thing is to love others like yourself, that's the chief thing, and that's everything; nothing else is wanted — you will find out at once how to arrange it all. And yet it's an old truth which has been told and retold a billion times — but it has not formed part of our lives! The consciousness of life is higher than life, the knowledge of the laws of happiness is higher than happiness — that is what one must contend against. And I shall. If only everyone wants it, it can be arranged at once.

And I tracked down that little girl . . . and I shall go on and on!

Bobok*
From Somebody's Diary†

Semyon Ardalyonovitch said to me all of a sudden the day before yesterday: "Why, will you ever be sober, Ivan Ivanovitch? Tell me that, pray."

A strange requirement. I did not resent it, I am a timid man; but here they have actually made me out mad. An artist painted my portrait as it happened: "After all, you are a literary man," he said. I submitted, he exhibited it. I read: "Go and look at that morbid face suggesting insanity."

It may be so, but think of putting it so bluntly into print. In print everything ought to be decorous; there ought to be ideals, while instead of that...

Say it indirectly, at least; that's what you have style for. But no, he doesn't care to do it indirectly. Nowadays humor and a fine style have disappeared, and abuse is accepted as wit. I do not resent it: but God

---

* A Bobok is a small bean.
† Translated by Constance Garnett.

knows I am not enough of a literary man to go out of my mind. I have written a novel, it has not been published. I have written articles — they have been refused. Those articles I took about from one editor to another; everywhere they refused them: you have no salt they told me. "What sort of salt do you want?" I asked with a leer. "Attic salt?"

They did not even understand, For the most part I translate from the French for the booksellers. I write advertisements for shopkeepers too: "Unique opportunity! Fine tea, from our own plantations . . ." I made a nice little sum over a panegyric on his deceased excellency Pyotr Matveyitch. I compiled the "Art of pleasing the ladies," a commission from a bookseller. I have brought out some six little works of this kind in the course of my life. I am thinking of making a collection of the bons mots of Voltaire, but am afraid it may seem a little flat to our people. Voltaire's no good now; nowadays we want a cudgel, not Voltaire. We knock each other's last teeth out nowadays. Well, so that's the whole extent of my literary activity. Though indeed I do send round letters to the editors gratis and fully signed. I give them all sorts of counsels and admonitions, criticize and point out the true path. The letter I sent last week to an editor's office was the fortieth I had sent in the last two years. I have wasted four rubles over stamps alone for them. My temper is at the bottom of it all.

I believe that the artist who painted me did so not for the sake of literature, but for the sake of two symmetrical warts on my forehead, a natural phenomenon, he would say. They have no ideas, so now they are out for phenomena. And didn't he succeed in getting my warts in his portrait — to the life. That is what they call realism.

And as to madness, a great many people were put

down as mad among us last year. And in such language! "With such original talent. . . . and yet, after all, it appears" . . . "however, one ought to have foreseen it long ago." That is rather artful; so that from the point of view of pure art one may really commend it. Well, but after all, these so-called madmen have turned out cleverer than ever. So it seems the critics can call them mad, but they cannot produce anyone better.

The wisest of all, in my opinion, is he who can, if only once a month, call himself a fool — a faculty unheard of nowadays. In old days, once a year at any rate a fool would recognize that he was a fool, but nowadays not a bit of it. And they have so muddled things up that there is no telling a fool from a wise man. They have done that on purpose.

I remember a witty Spaniard saying when, two hundred and fifty years ago, the French built their first madhouses: "They have shut up all their fools in a house apart, to make sure that they are wise men themselves." Just so: you don't show your own wisdom by shutting someone else in a madhouse. "K. has gone out of his mind, means that we are sane now." No, it doesn't mean that yet.

Hang it though, why am I maundering on? I go on grumbling and grumbling. Even my maidservant is sick of me. Yesterday a friend came to see me. "Your style is changing," he said; "it is choppy: you chop and chop — and then a parenthesis, then a parenthesis in the parenthesis, then you stick in something else in brackets, then you begin chopping and chopping again."

The friend is right. Something strange is happening to me. My character is changing and my head aches. I am beginning to see and hear strange things, not voices exactly, but as though someone beside me were muttering, "bobok, bobok, bobok!"

What's the meaning of this bobok? I must divert my mind.

I went out in search of diversion, I hit upon a funeral. A distant relation — a collegiate counselor, however. A widow and five daughters, all marriageable young ladies. What must it come to even to keep them in slippers. Their father managed it, but now there is only a little pension. They will have to eat humble pie. They have always received me ungraciously. And indeed I should not have gone to the funeral now had it not been for a peculiar circumstance. I followed the procession to the cemetery with the rest; they were stuck-up and held aloof from me. My uniform was certainly rather shabby. It's five-and-twenty years, I believe, since I was at the cemetery; what a wretched place!

To begin with the smell. There were fifteen hearses, with palls varying in expensiveness; there were actually two catafalques. One was a general's and one some lady's. There were many mourners, a great deal of feigned mourning and a great deal of open gaiety. The clergy have nothing to complain of; it brings them a good income. But the smell, the smell. I should not like to be one of the clergy here.

I kept glancing at the faces of the dead cautiously, distrusting my impressionability. Some had a mild expression, some looked unpleasant. As a rule the smiles were disagreeable, and in some cases very much so. I don't like them; they haunt one's dreams.

During the service I went out of the church into the air: it was a grey day, but dry. It was cold too, but then it was October. I walked about among the tombs. They are of different grades. The third grade cost thirty rubles; it's decent and not so very dear. The first two grades are tombs in the church and under the porch; they cost a pretty penny. On this occasion they were burying in tombs of the third grade six persons, among them the general and the lady.

I looked into the graves — and it was horrible: water and such water! Absolutely green, and . . . but there, why talk of it! The gravedigger was baling it out every minute. I went out while the service was going on and strolled outside the gates. Close by was an almshouse, and a little further off there was a restaurant. It was not a bad little restaurant: there was lunch and everything. There were lots of the mourners here. I noticed a great deal of gaiety and genuine heartiness. I had something to eat and drink.

Then I took part in the bearing of the coffin from the church to the grave. Why is it that corpses in their coffins are so heavy? They say it is due to some sort of inertia, that the body is no longer directed by its owner . . . or some nonsense of that sort, in opposition to the laws of mechanics and common sense. I don't like to hear people who have nothing but a general education venture to solve the problems that require special knowledge; and with us that's done continually. Civilians love to pass opinions about subjects that are the province of the soldier and even of the field-marshal; while men who have been educated as engineers prefer discussing philosophy and political economy.

I did not go to the requiem service. I have some pride, and if I am only received owing to some special necessity, why force myself on their dinners, even if it be a funeral dinner. The only thing I don't understand is why I stayed at the cemetery; I sat on a tombstone and sank into appropriate reflections.

I began with the Moscow exhibition and ended with reflecting upon astonishment in the abstract. My deductions about astonishment were these:

"To be surprised at everything is stupid of course, and to be astonished at nothing is a great deal more becoming and for some reason accepted as good form. But that is not really true. To my mind to be astonished at nothing is much more stupid than to be astonished at everything. And, moreover, to be astonished at nothing is almost the same as feeling respect for nothing. And indeed a stupid man is incapable of feeling respect."

"But what I desire most of all is to feel respect. I thirst to feel respect," one of my acquaintances said to me the other day.

He thirsts to feel respect! Goodness, I thought, what would happen to you if you dared to print that nowadays? At that point I sank into forgetfulness. I don't like reading the epitaphs of tombstones: they are everlastingly the same. An unfinished sandwich was lying on the tombstone near me; stupid and inappropriate. I threw it on the ground, as it was not bread but only a sandwich. Though I believe it is not a sin to throw bread on the earth, but only on the floor. I must look it up in Suvorin's calendar.

I suppose I sat there a long time — too long a time, in fact; I must have lain down on a long stone which was of the shape of a marble coffin. And how it happened I don't know, but I began to hear things of all sorts being said. At first I did not pay attention to it, but treated it with contempt. But the conversation went on. I heard muffled sounds as though the speakers' mouths were covered with a pillow, and at the same time they were distinct and very near. I came to myself, sat up and began listening attentively.

"Your Excellency, it's utterly impossible. You led hearts, I return your lead, and here you play the seven of diamonds. You ought to have given me a hint about diamonds."

"What, play by hard and fast rules? Where is the charm of that?"

"You must, your Excellency. One can't do anything without something to go upon. We must play with dummy, let one hand not be turned up."

"Well, you won't find a dummy here."

What conceited words! And it was queer and unexpected. One was such a ponderous, dignified voice, the other softly suave; I should not have believed it if I had not heard it myself. I had not been to the requiem dinner, I believe. And yet how could they be playing preference here and what general was this? That the sounds came from under the tombstones of that there could be no doubt. I bent down and read on the tomb:

"Here lies the body of Major-General Pervoyedov... a cavalier of such and such orders." Hm! "Passed away in August of this year... fifty-seven.... Rest, beloved ashes, till the joyful dawn!"

Hm, dash it, it really is a general! There was no monument on the grave from which the obsequious voice came, there was only a tombstone. He must have been a fresh arrival. From his voice he was a lower court councilor.

"Oh-ho-ho-ho!" I heard in a new voice a dozen yards from the general's resting-place, coming from quite a fresh grave. The voice belonged to a man and a plebeian, mawkish with its affectation of religious fervor. "Oh-ho-ho-ho!"

"Oh, here he is hiccupping again!" cried the haughty and disdainful voice of an irritated lady, apparently of the highest society. "It is an affliction to be by this shopkeeper!"

"I didn't hiccup; why, I've had nothing to eat. It's simply my nature. Really, madam, you don't seem able to get rid of your caprices here."

"Then why did you come and lie down here?"

"They put me here, my wife and little children put me here, I did not lie down here of myself. The mystery of death! And I would not have lain down beside you not for any money; I lie here as befitting my fortune, judging by the price. For we can always do that — pay for a tomb of the third grade."

"You made money, I suppose? You fleeced people?"

"Fleece you, indeed! We haven't seen the color of your money since January. There's a little bill against you at the shop."

"Well, that's really stupid; to try and recover debts here is too stupid, to my thinking! Go to the surface. Ask my niece — she is my heiress."

"There's no asking anyone now, and no going anywhere. We have both reached our limit and, before the judgment-seat of God, are equal in our sins."

"In our sins," the lady mimicked him contemptuously. "Don't dare to speak to me."

"Oh-ho-ho-ho!"

"You see, the shopkeeper obeys the lady, your Excellency."

"Why shouldn't he?"

"Why, your Excellency, because, as we all know, things are different here."

"Different? How?"

"We are dead, so to speak, your Excellency."

"Oh, yes! But still . . ."

Well, this is an entertainment, it is a fine show, I must say! If it has come to this down here, what can one expect on the surface? But what a queer business! I went on listening, however, though with extreme indignation.

"Yes, I should like a taste of life! Yes, you know . . . I should like a taste of fife." I heard a new voice suddenly somewhere in the space between the general and the irritable lady.

"Do you hear, your Excellency, our friend is at the same game again. For three days at a time he says nothing, and then he bursts out with 'I should like a taste of life, yes, a taste of life!' And with such appetite, he-he!"

"And such frivolity."

"It gets hold of him, your Excellency, and do you know, he is growing sleepy, quite sleepy — he has been here since April; and then all of a sudden 'I should like a taste of life!'"

"It is rather dull, though," observed his Excellency.

"It is, your Excellency. Shall we tease Avdotya Ignatyevna again, he-he?"

"No, spare me, please. I can't endure that quarrelsome virago."

"And I can't endure either of you," cried the virago disdainfully. "You are both of you bores and can't tell me anything ideal. I know one little story about you, your Excellency — don't turn up your nose, please — how a manservant swept you out from under a married couple's bed one morning."

"Nasty woman," the general muttered through his teeth.

"Avdotya Ignatycvna, ma'am," the shopkeeper wailed suddenly again, "my dear lady, don't be angry, but tell me, am I going through the ordeal by torment now, or is it something else?"

"Ah, he is at it again, as I expected! For there's a smell from him which means he is turning round!"

"I am not turning round, ma'am, and there's no particular smell from me, for I've kept my body whole as it should be, while you're regularly high. For the smell is really horrible even for a place like this. I don't speak of it, merely from politeness."

"Ah, you horrid, insulting wretch. He positively stinks and talks about me."

"Oh-ho-ho-ho! If only the time for my requiem would come quickly: I should hear their tearful voices over my head, my wife's lament and my children's soft weeping...!"

"Well, that's a thing to fret for! They'll stuff themselves with funeral rice and go home.... Oh, I wish somebody would wake up!"

"Avdotya Ignatyevna," said the insinuating government clerk, "wait a bit, the new arrivals will speak."

"And are there any young people among them?"

"Yes, there are, Avdotya Ignatyevna. There are some not more than lads."

"Oh, how welcome that would be!"

"Haven't they begun yet?" inquired his Excellency.

"Even those who came the day before yesterday haven't awakened yet, your Excellency. As you know, they sometimes don't speak for a week. It's a good job that today and yesterday and the day before they brought a whole lot. As it is, they are all last year's for seventy feet round."

"Yes, it will be interesting."

"Yes, your Excellency, they buried Tarasevitch, the privy councilor, today. I knew it from the voices. I know his nephew, he helped to lower the coffin just now."

"Hm, where is he, then?"

"Five steps from you, your Excellency, on the left.... Almost at your feet. You should make his acquaintance, your Excellency."

"Hm, no — it's not for me to make advances."

"Oh, he will begin of himself, your Excellency. He will be flattered. Leave it to me, your Excellency, and I..."

"Oh, oh...! What is happening to me?" croaked the frightened voice of a new arrival.

"A new arrival, your Excellency, a new arrival, thank

God! And how quick he's been! Sometimes they don't say a word for a week."

"Oh, I believe it's a young man!" Avdotya Ignatyevna cried shrilly.

"I . . . I . . . it was a complication, and so sudden!" faltered the young man again. "Only the evening before, Schultz said to me, 'There's a complication,' and I died suddenly before morning. Oh! oh!"

"Well, there's no help for it, young man," the general observed graciously, evidently pleased at a new arrival. "You must be comforted. You are kindly welcome to our Vale of Jehoshaphat, so to call it. We are kindhearted people, you will come to know us and appreciate us. Major-General Vassili Vassilitch Pervoyedov, at your service."

"Oh, no, no! Certainly not! I was at Schultz's; I had a complication, you know, at first it was my chest and a cough, and then I caught a cold: my lungs and influenza . . . and all of a sudden, quite unexpectedly . . . the worst of all was its being so unexpected."

"You say it began with the chest," the government clerk put in suavely, as though he wished to reassure the new arrival.

"Yes, my chest and catarrh and then no catarrh, but still the chest, and I couldn't breathe . . . and you know . . ."

"I know, I know. But if it was the chest you ought to have gone to Ecke and not to Schultz."

"You know, I kept meaning to go to Botkin's, and all at once . . ."

"Botkin is quite prohibitive," observed the general.

"Oh, no, he is not forbidding at all; I've heard he is so attentive and foretells everything beforehand."

"His Excellency was referring to his fees," the government clerk corrected him.

"Oh, not at all, he only asks three rubles, and he

makes such an examination, and gives you a prescription... and I was very anxious to see him, for I have been told... Well, gentlemen, had I better go to Ecke or to Botkin?"

"What? To whom?" The general's corpse shook with agreeable laughter. The government clerk echoed it in falsetto.

"Dear boy, dear, delightful boy, how I love you!" Avdotya Ignatyevna squealed ecstatically. "I wish they had put someone like you next to me."

No, that was too much! And these were the dead of our times! Still, I ought to listen to more and not be in too great a hurry to draw conclusions. That sniveling new arrival — I remember him just now in his coffin — had the expression of a frightened chicken, the most revolting expression in the world! However, let us wait and see.

But what happened next was such a Bedlam that I could not keep it all in my memory. For a great many woke up at once; an official — a civil councilor — woke up, and began discussing at once the project of a new sub-committee in a government department and of the probable transfer of various functionaries in connection with the sub-committee — which very greatly interested the general. I must confess I learnt a great deal that was new myself, so much so that I marveled at the channels by which one may sometimes in the metropolis learn government news. Then an engineer half woke up, but for a long time muttered absolute nonsense, so that our friends left off worrying him and let him lie till he was ready. At last the distinguished lady who had been buried in the morning under the catafalque showed symptoms of the reanimation of the tomb. Lebeziatnikov (for the obsequious lower court councilor whom I detested and who lay beside General Pervoyedov was called, it appears, Lebeziatnikov) became much excited, and surprised that they were all waking up so soon this time. I must own I was surprised too; though some of those who woke had been buried for three days, as, for instance, a very young girl of sixteen who kept giggling . . . giggling in a horrible and predatory way.

"Your Excellency, privy councilor Tarasevitch is waking!" Lebeziatnikov announced with extreme fussiness.

"Eh? What?" the privy councilor, waking up suddenly mumbled, with a lisp of disgust. There was a note of ill-humored peremptoriness in the sound of his voice.

I listened with curiosity — for during the last few days I had heard something about Tarasevitch — shocking and upsetting in the extreme.

"It's I, your Excellency, so far only I."

"What is your petition? What do you want?"

"Merely to inquire after your Excellency's health; in these unaccustomed surroundings everyone feels at first, as it were, oppressed. General Pervoyedov wishes to have the honor of making your Excellency's acquaintance, and hopes . . ."

"I've never heard of him."

"Surely, your Excellency! General Pervoyedov, Vassili Vassilitch . . ."

"Are you General Pervoyedov?"

"No, your Excellency, I am only the lower court councilor Lebeziatnikov, at your service, but General Pervoyedov . . ."

"Nonsense! And I beg you to leave me alone."

"Let him be." General Pervoyedov at last himself checked with dignity the disgusting officiousness of his sycophant in the grave.

"He is not fully awake, your Excellency, you must consider that; it's the novelty of it all. When he is fully awake he will take it differently."

"Let him be," repeated the general.

"Vassili Vassilitch! Hey, your Excellency!" a perfectly new voice shouted loudly and aggressively from close beside Avdotya Ignatyevna. It was a voice of gentlemanly insolence, with the languid pronunciation now fashionable and an arrogant drawl. "I've been watching you all for the last two hours. Do you remember me, Vassili Vassilitch? My name is Klinevitch, we met at the Volokonskys' where you, too, were received as a guest, I am sure I don't know why."

"What, Count Pyotr Petrovitch. . . ? Can it be really you . . . and at such an early age? How sorry I am to hear it."

"Oh, I am sorry myself, though I really don't mind, and I want to amuse myself as far as I can everywhere. And I am not a count but a baron, only a baron. We are only a set of scurvy barons, risen from being flunkeys, but why I don't know and I don't care. I am only a scoundrel of the pseudo-aristocratic society, and I am regarded as 'a charming polisson.' My father is a wretched little general, and my mother was at one time received en haut lieu. With the help of the Jew Zifel I forged fifty thousand ruble notes last year and then I informed against him, while Julie Charpentier de Lusignan carried off the money to Bordeaux. And only fancy, I was engaged to be married — to a girl still at school, three months under sixteen, with a dowry of ninety thousand. Avdotya Ignatyevna, do you remember how you seduced me fifteen years ago when I was a boy of fourteen in the Corps des Pages?"

"Ah, that's you, you rascal! Well, you are a godsend, anyway, for here. . . ."

"You were mistaken in suspecting your neighbor, the business gentleman, of unpleasant fragrance. . . . I said nothing, but I laughed. The stench came from me: they had to bury me in a nailed-up coffin."

"Ugh, you horrid creature! Still, I am glad you are here; you can't imagine the lack of life and wit here."

"Quite so, quite so, and I intend to start here something original. Your Excellency — I don't mean you, Pervoyedov — your Excellency the other one, Tarasevitch, the privy councilor! Answer! I am Klinevitch, who took you to Mlle. Furie in Lent, do you hear?"

"I do, Klinevitch, and I am delighted, and trust me
.

"I wouldn't trust you with a halfpenny, and I don't care. I simply want to kiss you, dear old man, but luckily I can't. Do you know, gentlemen, what this grand-pere's little game was? He died three or four days ago, and would you believe it, he left a deficit of four hundred thousand government money from the fund for widows and orphans. He was the sole person in control of it for some reason, so that his accounts were not audited for the last eight years. I can fancy what long faces they all have now, and what they call him. It's a delectable thought, isn't it? I have been wondering for the last year how a wretched old man of seventy, gouty and rheumatic, succeeded in preserving the physical energy for his debaucheries — and now the riddle is solved! Those widows and orphans — the very thought of them must have egged him on! I knew about it long ago, I was the only one who did know; it was Julie told me, and as soon as I discovered it, I attacked him in a friendly way at once in Easter week: 'Give me twenty-five thousand, if you don't they'll look into your accounts tomorrow.' And just fancy, he had only thirteen thousand left then, so it seems it was very apropos his dying now. Grand-pere, grand-pere; do you hear?"

"Cher Khnevitch, I quite agree with you, and there was no need for you . . . to go into such details. Life is so full of suffering and torment and so little to make up for it . . . that I wanted at last to be at rest, and so far as I can see I hope to get all I can from here too."

"I bet that he has already sniffed Katiche Berestoy!"

"Who? What Katiche?" There was a rapacious quiver in the old man's voice.

"A-ah, what Katiche? Why, here on the left, five paces from me and ten from you. She has been here for five days, and if only you knew, grand-pere, what a little wretch she is! Of good family and breeding and a monster, a regular monster! I did not introduce her to anyone there, I was the only one who knew her. . . . Katiche, answer!"

"He-he-he!" the girl responded with a jangling laugh, in which there was a note of something as sharp as the prick of a needle. "He-he-he!"

"And a little blonde?" the grand-pere faltered, drawling out the syllables.

"He-he-he!"

"I . . . have long . . . I have long," the old man faltered breathlessly, "cherished the dream of a little fair thing of fifteen and just in such surroundings."

"Ach, the monster!" cried Avdotya Ignatyevna.

"Enough!" Klinevitch decided. "I see there is excellent material. We shall soon arrange things better. The great thing is to spend the rest of our time cheerfully; but what time? Hey, you, government clerk, Lebeziatnikov or whatever it is, I hear that's your name!"

"Semyon Yevseitch Lebeziatnikov, lower court councilor, at your service, very, very, very much delighted to meet you."

"I don't care whether you are delighted or not, but you seem to know everything here. Tell me first of all how it is we can talk? I've been wondering ever since yesterday. We are dead and yet we are talking and seem to be moving — and yet we are not talking and not moving. What jugglery is this?"

"If you want an explanation, baron, Platon Nikolaevitch could give you one better than I."

"What Platon Nikolaevitch is that? To the point. Don't beat about the bush."

"Platon Nikolaevitch is our home-grown philosopher, scientist and Master of Arts. He has brought out several philosophical works, but for the last three months he has been getting quite drowsy, and there is no stirring him up now. Once a week he mutters something utterly irrelevant."

"To the point, to the point!"

"He explains all this by the simplest fact, namely, that when we were living on the surface we mistakenly thought that death there was death. The body revives, as it were, here, the remains of life are concentrated, but only in consciousness. I don't know how to express it, but life goes on, as it were, by inertia. In his opinion everything is concentrated somewhere in consciousness and goes on for two or three months . . . sometimes even for half a year. . . . There is one here, for instance, who is almost completely decomposed, but once every six weeks he suddenly utters one word, quite senseless of course, about some bobok, 'Bobok, bobok,' but you see that an imperceptible speck of life is still warm within him."

"It's rather stupid. Well, and how is it I have no sense of smell and yet I feel there's a stench?"

"That . . . he-he . . . Well, on that point our philosopher is a bit foggy. It's apropos of smell, he said, that the stench one perceives here is, so to speak, moral — he-he! It's the stench of the soul, he says, that in these two or three months it may have time to recover itself . . . and this is, so to speak, the last mercy. . . . Only, I think, baron, that these are mystic ravings very excusable in his position . . .

"Enough; all the rest of it, I am sure, is nonsense. The great thing is that we have two or three months more of life and then — bobok! I propose to spend these two months as agreeably as possible, and so to arrange everything on a new basis. Gentlemen! I propose to cast aside all shame."

"Ah, let us cast aside all shame, let us!" many voices could be heard saying; and strange to say, several new voices were audible, which must have belonged to others newly awakened. The engineer, now fully awake, boomed out his agreement with peculiar delight. The girl Katiche giggled gleefully.

"Oh, how I long to cast off all shame!" Avdotya Ignatyevna exclaimed rapturously.

"I say, if Avdotya Ignatyevna wants to cast off all shame . . ."

"No, no, no, Klinevitch, I was ashamed up there all the same, but here I should like to cast off shame, I should like it awfully."

"I understand, Klinevitch," boomed the engineer, "that you want to rearrange life here on new and rational principles."

"Oh, I don't care a hang about that! For that we'll wait for Kudeyarov who was brought here yesterday. When he wakes he'll tell you all about it. He is such a personality, such a titanic personality! Tomorrow they'll bring along another natural scientist, I believe, an officer for certain, and three or four days later a journalist, and, I believe, his editor with him. But deuce take them all, there will be a little group of us anyway, and things will arrange themselves. Though meanwhile I don't want us to be telling lies. That's all I care about, for that is one thing that matters. One cannot exist on the surface without lying, for life and lying are synonymous, but here we will amuse ourselves by not lying. Hang it all, the grave has some value after all! We'll all tell our stories aloud, and we won't be ashamed of anything. First of all I'll tell you about myself. I am one of the predatory kind, you know. All that was bound and held in check by rotten cords up there on the surface. Away with cords and let us spend these two months in shameless truthfulness! Let us strip and be naked!"

"Let us be naked, let us be naked!" cried all the voices.

"I long to be naked, I long to be," Avdotya Ignatyevna shrilled.

"Ah . . . ah, I see we shall have fun here; I don't want Ecke after all."

"No, I tell you. Give me a taste of life!"

"He-he-he!" giggled Katiche.

"The great thing is that no one can interfere with us, and though I see Pervoyedov is in a temper, he can't reach me with his hand. Grand-pere, do you agree?"

"I fully agree, fully, and with the utmost satisfaction, but on condition that Katiche is the first to give us her biography."

"I protest! I protest with all my heart!" General Pervoyedov brought out firmly.

"Your Excellency!" the scoundrel Lebeziatnikov persuaded him in a murmur of fussy excitement, "your Excellency, it will be to our advantage to agree. Here, you see, there's this girl's . . . and all their little affairs."

"There's the girl, it's true, but . . ."

"It's to our advantage, your Excellency, upon my word it is! If only as an experiment, let us try it . . ."

"Even in the grave they won't let us rest in peace."

"In the first place, General, you were playing preference in the grave, and in the second we don't care a hang about you," drawled Klinevitch.

"Sir, I beg you not to forget yourself."

"What? Why, you can't get at me, and I can tease you from here as though you were Julie's lapdog. And another thing, gentlemen, how is he a general here? He was a general there, but here is mere refuse."

"No, not mere refuse. . . . Even here . . ."

"Here you will rot in the grave and six brass buttons will be all that will be left of you."

"Bravo, Klinevitch, ha-ha-ha!" roared voices.

"I have served my sovereign. . . . I have the sword . . ."

"Your sword is only fit to prick mice, and you never drew it even for that."

"That makes no difference; I formed a part of the whole."

"There are all sorts of parts in a whole."

"Bravo, Klinevitch, bravo! Ha-ha-ha!"

"I don't understand what the sword stands for," boomed the engineer.

"We shall run away from the Prussians like mice, they'll crush us to powder!" cried a voice in the distance that was unfamiliar to me, that was positively spluttering with glee.

"The sword, sir, is an honor," the general cried, but only I heard him. There arose a prolonged and furious roar, clamor, and hubbub, and only the hysterically impatient squeals of Avdotya Ignatyevna were audible.

"But do let us make haste! Ah, when are we going to begin to cast off all shame!"

"Oh-ho-ho. . . ! The soul does in truth pass through torments!" exclaimed the voice of the plebeian, "and . . ."

And here I suddenly sneezed. It happened suddenly and unintentionally, but the effect was striking: all became as silent as one expects it to be in a churchyard, it all vanished like a dream. A real silence of the tomb set in. I don't believe they were ashamed on account of my presence: they had made up their minds to cast off all shame! I waited five minutes — not a word, not a sound. It cannot be supposed that they were afraid of my informing the police; for what could the police do to them? I must conclude that they had some secret unknown to the living, which they carefully concealed from every mortal.

"Well, my dears," I thought, "I shall visit you again." And with those words, I left the cemetery.

No, that I cannot admit; no, I really cannot! The bobok case does not trouble me (so that is what the bobok signified!)

Depravity in such a place, depravity of the last aspirations, depravity of sodden and rotten corpses — and not even sparing the last moments of consciousness! Those moments have been granted, vouchsafed to them, and . . . and, worst of all, in such a place! No, that I cannot admit.

I shall go to other tombs, I shall listen everywhere. Certainly one ought to listen everywhere and not merely at one spot in order to form an idea. Perhaps one may come across something reassuring.

But I shall certainly go back to those. They promised their biographies and anecdotes of all sorts. Tfoo! But I shall go, I shall certainly go; it is a question of conscience!

I shall take it to the *Citizen*; the editor there has had his portrait exhibited too. Maybe he will print it.

CPSIA information can be obtained
at www.ICGtesting.com
Printed in the USA
LVHW111929141022
730718LV00003B/395